# Frankley Library
## Balaam Wood School, New Street. B45 0EU
## Tel: 0121 464 7676

Loans are up to 28 days. Fines are charged if items are not returned by the due date. Items can be renewed at the Library, via the internet or by telephone up to 3 times.

Items in demand will not be renewed.

**Date for return**

D1495198

Check out our online catalogue to see what's in stock, renew or reserve books.

http://birmingham.spydus.co.uk

Like us on Facebook!

**Please use a bookmark.**

Birmingham
City Council

C2 000 004 740779

**Abby Green** got hooked on Mills & Boon® romances while still in her teens, when she stumbled across one belonging to her grandmother in the west of Ireland. After many years of reading them voraciously, she sat down one day and gave it a go herself. Happily, after a few failed attempts, Mills & Boon bought her first manuscript.

Abby works freelance in the film and TV industry, but thankfully the four a.m. starts and the stresses of dealing with recalcitrant actors are becoming more and more infrequent, leaving her more time to write!

She loves to hear from readers, and you can contact her through her website at www.abby-green.com. She lives and works in Dublin.

**Recent titles by the same author:**

ONE NIGHT WITH THE ENEMY
THE LEGEND OF DE MARCO
THE CALL OF THE DESERT
THE SULTAN'S CHOICE

**Did you know these are also available as eBooks?**
**Visit www.millsandboon.co.uk**

# EXQUISITE
# REVENGE

BY
## ABBY GREEN

First published in Great Britain 2012
by Mills & Boon, an imprint of Harlequin (UK) Limited.
Harlequin (UK) Limited, Eton House, 18-24 Paradise Road,
Richmond, Surrey TW9 1SR

© Abby Green 2012

ISBN: 978 0 263 89130 0

Harlequin (UK) policy is to use papers that are natural, renewable and recyclable products and made from wood grown in sustainable forests. The logging and manufacturing process conform to the legal environmental regulations of the country of origin.

Printed and bound in Spain
by Blackprint CPI, Barcelona

# EXQUISITE
# REVENGE

This is especially for my father Martin Green
who is a poet, scribe and playwright.
He was also a publisher and a biographer.
Thank you for passing onto me, a love of words
and books and a smidgeon of your talent.

# CHAPTER ONE

'Who is that?' Luc Sanchis's voice was artfully bored, belying his sudden irrational spiking of interest. The woman who had caught it wasn't even remotely his type.

'The short-haired strawberry-blonde?'

Luc nodded curtly, irritated that he'd even asked the question now, and by the fact that she'd caught his eye. Why? His solicitor knew him too well—knew that Luc never asked a question that wasn't utterly relevant in some way.

'That's Jesse Moriarty. Of JM Holdings.'

Luc frowned, taking in the slim figure of below average height. She was turned sideways to him through the thronged room, and unlike every other woman there was dressed in a dark grey trouser suit. She stood out precisely because she was dressed differently and because she looked acutely self-conscious on her own.

Even from here he could see the pained expression on her face and the almost white-knuckled grip on her glass of champagne—which she wasn't drinking. She was staring fixedly at something in the distance.

His solicitor must have assumed Luc hadn't heard of JM Holdings and was explaining. 'When she does decide to float it, the rumour is that it'll be worth upwards of fifty-five million. Not bad for someone who emerged onto the jaded IT scene just a few years ago.'

Luc asked now, 'What's her background?'

'She got a scholarship to Cambridge and while she was studying computer science and economics she patented the anti-hacking system that's now being used as the highest level of security within companies across the globe—not to mention your own company. Some say she's a genius.'

Luc's eyes narrowed on the slight figure. She didn't look like a genius. She looked lost, fragile. Alone in the crowd. He was surprised by a surge of something that felt curiously protective within him, as if he wanted to go over there and take her hand.

His solicitor was saying in a low voice, 'She's known by those who work for her as The Machine. In her personal dealings she's rumoured to be positively arctic—no mention of love affairs…my money says she's gay—'

His solicitor broke off as he was accosted by someone he knew; he shot Luc an apologetic glance as he was led away. Luc welcomed it. He didn't care for that kind of lazy commenting on women, and wasn't the kind of man who felt uncomfortable standing alone. He was aware of the sudden interest in the women nearby now that he *was* alone, but he still couldn't take his eyes off Jesse Moriarty.

He'd heard of JM Holdings. Of course he had. The supposedly unhackable security system she'd devised *was* genius. He'd just never imagined that the notoriously publicity-shy person behind JM Holdings would be this slight and very young-looking woman.

At that moment she broke her gaze from whatever she'd been staring at and turned to face towards where Luc stood. His whole body tensed. In contrast to the slightly mannish clothes she wore she had a pretty face: heart-shaped, with huge eyes. She looked pale, slightly shellshocked. He saw her put the still full glass onto a passing waiter's tray and she started to move towards him through the crowd.

He could see as she came closer that she wore a white shirt under her jacket. The look was very classic and cool, and yet utterly unfeminine—especially compared to the women decked out in *haute couture* finery around her. It was as if she'd wandered into the wrong place, and yet the intent in her expression told him she was definitely in the right place.

She was so close now that he could see just how tense she was, the faint sheen of perspiration on her brow. She wore no make-up, but she didn't need it with that perfect skin, and that made a jolt of awareness run through his body. He couldn't remember the last time he'd seen a woman with no make-up. It was curiously intimate.

Luc didn't move a fraction, but as Jesse Moriarty came alongside where he stood someone stepped backwards into her path and she pitched sideways helplessly. Luc's hands had stretched out even before he knew what he was doing and wrapped around slender upper arms.

Huge eyes widened and stared up into his. They were so dark grey they looked almost navy blue, and for a second Luc forgot everything. Who he was. Where he was. All he could see were those huge eyes and this woman under his hands. He saw two pink flags of colour come into her cheeks, the way her eyes darkened even more. There was something so inexplicably appealing about her that it snuck right under the iron-clad guard Luc had built up over years, which had become like a second skin… When he realised that he jerked back, all but thrusting her away from him as he did so.

He was reacting on a very deep and primitive level to this moment and to how effortlessly she'd managed to enthral him. The only women who enthralled him were women he *allowed* to enthral him. There was little that was spontaneous about it. So this whole bizarre interlude with a complete relative stranger made his voice unintentionally harsh. 'You should watch where you're going.'

He saw hurt and chagrin flare in those huge eyes before her expression cleared and became completely cold. The words of his solicitor came back to him: *positively arctic*.

She stepped back. Her eyes darted up and down once, quickly, and then she said with a husky tone which caught at Luc's pulse, 'It was an accident.'

The look she left him with could have frozen over the Sahara. And then she disappeared into the heaving throng and Luc had an even more curious impulse to snatch her back and—*what*? Apologise? His conscience mocked him. Was he getting soft in his old age? He knew well that the women who populated his world, whether they be business colleagues or more mercenary types searching for a rich meal ticket, were not vulnerable creatures who wore their hearts on their sleeves or in their huge expressive eyes. Oh, he knew those kind of women existed, but more often than not they were an illusion designed to entrap. He had been entrapped once. But never again.

When he recalled the way Jesse Moriarty had frozen him out so effectively he knew for a fact that she was one of the most *in*vulnerable kind. So why was it so hard for him to get those huge eyes and that slight figure in the unflattering suit out of his mind?

*One Year Later...*

'Just what exactly is your interest in JP O'Brien Construction, Mr Sanchis?'

Luc Sanchis sat back in his chair and regarded the bristling woman in front of him, who had just marched into his office as if she owned it and now stood with her hands on his desk, chin stuck forward pugnaciously. The fact that *no one* ever did this caused a frisson of surprise to run through him.

It had been one year since he'd seen her, and in that year

the huge eyes which were looking at him now, spitting dark grey sparks, had proved to be annoyingly memorable. But he was realising that his imagination didn't live up to reality.

Irritation surged at the unwelcome reminder of momentary human weakness. Even though this was only their second meeting Jesse Moriarty was proving to have a knack for rubbing him up the wrong way. He too stood and placed his hands on his desk, effortlessly asserting his vastly superior height and strength.

'*Ms* Moriarty, I suggest that you sit down if you want this conversation to go any further.'

Across the wide oak desk Jesse looked into brown eyes so dark they looked black, and just like last year, when she'd bumped into him at that function, she felt as if she were losing her balance.

The emotional turmoil that had galvanised her to come here and confront him seemed to dissipate, leaving her feeling shaky and very aware of her surroundings. She straightened up and then sat down abruptly in the chair behind her.

She watched as Luc Sanchis took his hands off the desk and sat down too, not taking those remarkable eyes off her for a second. All of a sudden Jesse felt boiling hot in her buttoned-up shirt and jumper. She'd only realised who he was when she'd seen him in a newspaper a few months ago and had put a name to the enigmatic stranger she'd bumped into at that function. The fact that his features had been memorable enough for that to happen had been very disconcerting.

*Luc Sanchis*.

He was half-French, half-Spanish. CEO of Sanchis Construction & Design, one of the most successful construction/architect design hybrid companies in the world. He was renowned globally for marrying innovative design with cutting edge, environmentally friendly construction practices.

She remembered how exposed she'd felt when he'd looked

into her eyes more deeply than anyone ever had before. The cool distance she'd surrounded herself with for years had spectacularly deserted her for precious seconds when he'd caught her in his hands. She'd felt the brand of those hands on her arms for days afterwards. More disturbingly, she'd not been able to forget her curious hurt when he'd practically thrust her away from him, as if the very sight of her had repulsed him.

He was on his phone now, speaking in a deep, lightly accented voice, instructing his assistant to bring in some refreshments. She wanted to tell him not to bother with refreshments but she was afraid to speak; emotion was still high in her chest and she wanted to gather herself, not give him a hint of how badly he upset her equilibrium. Now and a year ago.

He put down the phone, those eyes still dark and unnerving. Unreadable.

'So, Ms Moriarty, why don't we start again?'

Jesse bristled at his tone, but quashed her reaction and forced words out. 'Forgive me. I didn't mean to appear rude.'

He arched a brow and she heard a noise which heralded the arrival of his assistant with a tray holding coffee. She welcomed the momentary respite and watched Luc Sanchis as he accepted coffee with a smile. Her heart kicked. His dark olive-skinned features were more rugged than prettily handsome, and that realisation sent a shockwave of sensation through the tense core of her body.

The assistant left and Jesse took a sip of coffee, willing her hand not to tremble. She put the cup back down, looked at Luc Sanchis and steeled herself.

'I'd like to know what your interest is in JP O'Brien Construction.'

He put down his own cup and sat back in his big leather chair, steepling his hands over his chest. His shoulders were impossibly broad, and the white shirt and silk tie only gave the illusion of civility. Raw masculinity oozed from this man like a tangible force. It made Jesse feel very prickly.

'With all due respect,' he pointed out, 'I don't think that's any of your business.'

He might as well have inserted the word *damn* into that sentence.

'I think a far more pertinent question here, Ms Moriarty, is why the hell do you care about my interest in O'Brien Construction?'

*Why indeed?* Jesse was feeling pinned under his intent gaze, and it got worse when he sat forward. She stood up jerkily, needing to put some space between them. She never lost her cool like this. She had a reputation for being preternaturally collected. She grimaced inwardly. Along with a less flattering reputation for being emotionless. But in the past week all she seemed to have been feeling *was* emotions, and one very turbulent one in particular—which had led her here to this man's office.

Agitated, Jesse walked over to the wall of windows which took in an astounding view of the London skyline. She could feel Luc Sanchis's gaze boring into her back like a laser.

She heard movement behind her and then a very irritated sounding voice.

'Perhaps you have time on your hands to pose questions that are none of your business, but I don't.'

Jesse turned to see Luc Sanchis come around his desk and stand with an arm outstretched, indicating that she should leave. In that moment, to her absolute horror and chagrin, all she could see was his shirt pulled taut across his massive chest, the hard ridged muscles of his abdomen clearly delineated through the thin material.

Jesse was shocked to find herself so physically aware of a man she'd only recently discovered came with a reputed sexual prowess on a par with the world's most legendary lovers. His fierce privacy only compounded those rumours, but from where she was standing right now it was far too credible.

Forcing herself to get a grip, she focused on those black eyes. She had no intention of moving now—not when he was the only thing that stood between her and seeing JP O'Brien punished for his crimes. She'd worked too hard for this.

She took a deep breath. 'Whatever you're planning on investing in O'Brien to save him, I'm willing to match it.'

Luc Sanchis's arm dropped. His eyes narrowed and Jesse forced herself to stand strong. Now that she knew who he was, and just how powerful, she knew that if he was determined to save O'Brien then he would be an immovable force.

With a deceptively bland tone in his voice, which didn't fool Jesse for a second, he asked, 'Now, why on earth would JM Holdings, the most successful IT company to emerge in Europe for years, be interested in a construction company? Wasn't your last acquisition a gaming consortium?'

Jesse flushed uncomfortably and had to struggle not to look away for a second. The last thing she wanted was this man's far too incisive mind questioning her motives. She tried to disguise her rattled composure. 'My interest in O'Brien Construction is not up for discussion. You're either willing to let me match your offer or not.'

'And yet it's up for discussion when you want to find out *my* interests?'

Jesse flushed at having that glaring inconsistency pointed out. Something subtle changed in the air in that moment, and her skin puckered all over into goosebumps. Luc Sanchis had crossed his arms across that formidable chest and sat on the corner of his desk, one leg hitched up slightly. The material of his dark trousers stretched taut across one thigh, the awareness of which made Jesse's hands clench into fists at her sides.

Luc looked at the woman who stood so tensely across his office. He could almost see her quiver with it. He hated to admit it, because little piqued his interest these days, but she was intriguing him on a lot of levels after his initial shock in seeing her again.

Physically she wasn't his type at all, and yet he couldn't deny that, much as last year, something about her compelled him to keep looking at her. He preferred statuesque voluptuous beauties who were confident and experienced. Jesse Moriarty was petite and athletically slim. She more closely resembled a pale shadow than a sexually confident woman. Her figure was completely obscured in a conservative uniform of narrow charcoal-grey trousers, and a white silk shirt buttoned up underneath a jumper. Her hair was cut almost militarily short, the strawberry-blonde strands feathered close to her skull.

So why was it that Luc felt the irritating urge to deny the frisson of something hot in his bloodstream? He was a red-blooded, sexual man, so her very ascetic non-appeal should *not* be triggering a flare of sensation along his nerve-endings.

He frowned inwardly and told himself that it was the memory of his last lover that was heating his blood—not this woman who looked as if she'd prefer to jump out of his window than be here facing him. Not a reaction he was used to having from a woman. He wondered idly if his solicitor had been right; perhaps she *was* gay?

Jesse wished that Luc Sanchis would stop looking at her as if she was a specimen on a lab table. He opened his mouth to speak and her eye was effortlessly drawn to his sensuous lower lip. She wondered helplessly when she had ever noticed a man's mouth as being sensual before.

'Ms Moriarty, unless you're willing to give me an explanation as to why you don't want me to invest in O'Brien then I'm afraid this meeting is over. I don't deal in riddles.'

His voice rumbled through her and Jesse folded her arms across her chest tightly. Feeling unbelievably threatened, she blurted out, 'He's practically bankrupt…his business is in tatters…surely he has nothing to offer you?'

Luc Sanchis's mouth tightened. 'At the risk of repeating myself, once again I'm afraid the onus is on *you* to tell me why you're so interested in him.'

When Jesse was obstinately silent for a long moment he said, with an icy bite of reluctance, 'O'Brien still has stakes in Eastern European construction that I'm interested in acquiring before it's too late to salvage anything.' He shrugged one wide shoulder. 'If that means saving O'Brien in the process then so be it. You have to admit that I can claim a far more legitimate interest in his concerns than you.'

Jesse's brain hurt; what he said made perfect sense. At first she'd thought Luc Sanchis must be in league with O'Brien, but she'd checked him out and his reputation was pristine. Not a hint of misdeed or corruption, which an association with O'Brien might have indicated. And he had no previous connection to O'Brien. He'd literally come out of nowhere as a last-minute saviour.

Luc Sanchis shifted on the desk now, and Jesse felt his renewed interest with a shiver of foreboding down her spine.

'Why haven't you just gone directly to O'Brien with a better offer?'

Jesse paled, not wanting to remember her first face-to-face meeting with O'Brien the week before. She should have expected Luc Sanchis to ask the most logical question of all, but inside her head she was wondering hysterically what he would do if she was to blurt out the full, ugly and lurid truth of her relationship with O'Brien.

She avoided his eye. 'I have my reasons.' It was a pathetic non-answer, but she couldn't explain that, having confronted O'Brien once already, she couldn't approach him again. She'd burnt her bridges in that meeting but had only done it because she'd thought she was safe—that no one else would bail him out before it was too late.

The reason why she couldn't be cool and calm and answer Luc Sanchis's questions with logical answers was because this had nothing to do with business; this was about hurt and pain. Grief and suffering. And, above all, revenge. How could she even begin to make someone else understand the whirling cauldron of dark emotions inside her? She'd lived with this for so long...

Luc Sanchis unfolded his tall frame from the desk and stood up. Jesse couldn't help her gaze going to him, as if pulled against her will. His face was stern. He'd had enough.

'Whatever your mysterious reasons are, the question is this: who wants to invest in him more?'

Jesse could sense Luc Sanchis's intractability. She might be powerful in her own right, having built up a multi-million-pound IT software business, but she couldn't compete with this man if he chose to fight her.

She had to make him believe it didn't mean that much to her. When it meant *everything*.

'Look,' she said now, with a studied nonchalance that belied the thumping of her heart and the bead of sweat forming between her breasts, 'I'm willing to double the amount you've offered O'Brien if you'll drop your plans to invest.'

Luc stared at Jesse Moriarty. He didn't like the questions she was posing in his mind with this determination to match his offer—*more* than match it. She obviously desperately wanted O'Brien. Something inside him hardened. The problem was, so did he. He'd worked far too hard and long to let this opportunity pass. Especially not for some prickly slip of a woman who was starting seriously to irritate him with those huge eyes and the way colour flooded her cheeks so easily—as if she didn't knowingly use that to good effect.

Women like Jesse Moriarty didn't get to be successful in

business by being nice or kind. They were ruthless and single-minded and didn't care who they stepped on to get ahead. He'd learnt a valuable lesson early on at the hands of a woman determined to succeed at all costs, and he had no intention of letting Jesse Moriarty divert him from a path he'd set out on almost fifteen years before.

Resolutely he went towards her.

Jesse's eyes grew wide when she saw Luc Sanchis move. She had to consciously battle the urge not to take a step back. Her arms dropped and her hands clenched into fists again. She felt inordinately threatened by the sheer size and presence of the man. He was built more like an athlete than a titan of industry. All six foot four of him towered above her, and she wished for the umpteenth time that she was taller and more formidable.

He held out a hand and said with the utmost civility, 'You could quadruple the amount, Ms Moriarty, and I still wouldn't back down. If you do go to O'Brien with a higher bid, even if it's anonymous, I'll just match it until I've priced you out. I'm sorry your journey has been a wasted one today.'

# CHAPTER TWO

JESSE looked at Luc Sanchis's hand dumbly; he'd just confirmed her worst fear. He would thwart her no matter what.

She had a burning urge to get out of there now. With the utmost reluctance she lifted her hand and slipped it into his to shake it. The physical effect was instantaneous; it was like a nuclear reactor exploding deep inside her, sending a mushroom cloud of devastating sensation to the far corners of her body.

Like a scalded cat, she pulled her hand free, even though they'd touched for less than a second. She saw belatedly that Luc Sanchis was also holding out her slim briefcase from where she must have dropped it onto the floor near the desk. She hadn't even noticed and her cheeks burned. She grabbed it inelegantly and looked up at him, forcing her brain to work.

Stiffly she said, 'I'm sorry that I can't persuade you to re-think your plans to invest. Good day, Mr Sanchis.'

His voice took on a far more ambiguous tone. 'Don't be sorry. Meeting you was certainly…interesting.'

Mortification rushed through Jesse. *Interesting* felt like a slap in the face. She couldn't be further removed from this man's world, which she imagined to be peopled with all sorts of sensual pleasures and women to match. Never had she felt so gauche. Bitter gall rose in her throat, tasting of defeat, but she couldn't deal with that now—not in such close proximity to this man.

She turned and walked blindly to the door across what felt like acres and acres of dark grey carpet. The door was heavy, and it was only when it shut behind her with a quiet thud that she breathed in again, light-headed from holding her breath.

The rather austere-looking middle-aged secretary stood up to show her to the outer door, saying politely, 'Good day, Miss Moriarty, I trust you can find your way back to the lift?'

Jesse nodded and said her thanks. It was only when she'd stepped into the sleek lift to descend that the enormity of what had just happened and what it now meant hit her.

Luc stared at the closed door for an inordinately long moment. A delicate scent tickled his nostrils, and he realised it was *her* scent. It was somehow opulent and *sexy*. Totally at odds with the uptight image she portrayed. And yet the thought of that buttoned-up shirt sent a very unwelcome shot of desire through his lower body.

Luc scowled and shook his head, turning to face the spectacular view of London, digging his hands into his pockets. Jesse Moriarty was an enigma, all right, with her bizarre request for him not to invest in O'Brien Construction. What the hell was she up to? Why was it so important that she'd spend millions to stop him?

A disembodied voice came from the phone on his desk. 'Luc, the video conference call is ready. They're waiting in New York for you to join them.'

Luc turned and strode towards his desk. 'Thanks, Deborah, just give me a minute…'

As Luc shifted his mind from Jesse Moriarty with more difficulty than he'd like to admit, he recalled the way she'd visibly flinched away from the barest of contacts with his

hand. Definitely gay, he surmised, not liking the way something within him rebelled at that thought.

Cursing this uncharacteristic blip in his concentration, he
turned his attention to the next item on his agenda.

Jesse sat in a huge armchair which was positioned right in
front of the floor-to-ceiling window in her penthouse apartment. The view, much like the one in Luc Sanchis's office
today, encompassed London's city centre. Her legs were
curled up beneath her and she'd changed into loose sweats, a
tank top and a cashmere V-necked jumper. Her hands were
tightly clasped around a mug of tea. The rest of the apartment
around her was dark, the only light coming from her kitchen
which was off the main living area.

Jesse usually found this time of night and the view sooth-
ing. It always served to remind her of just how far she'd come:
from the monosyllabic, grief-stricken, traumatised child she'd
been to a woman who controlled a multi-million-pound company and who had been named Entrepreneur of the Year by
a leading financial establishment.

She'd been a young girl filled with blind rage and grief
who had discovered she could escape from real life into school
and do better than everyone around her. It hadn't earned her
any friends in the series of grim comprehensives she'd gone
to, but gradually she'd seen a way she could use her intelli-
gence to climb out of her challenged circumstances and had
earned a scholarship to university.

Her hatred had morphed into something more ambitious:
a desire to be able to stand in front of her father one day and
let him know that she was the architect of his downfall. To
let him know that she hadn't forgotten, and that he hadn't
escaped unscathed from the sins of his past. Jesse's mother
could have been saved if she'd received adequate medical

treatment in time, but her father had been too drunk and self-absorbed to care.

He'd killed her as effectively as if he'd done it with his own bare hands.

Jesse's hands tightened around her mug unconsciously as she recalled standing in front of her father last week. It had only been her second time seeing him in the flesh since she was a child. The first time had been at that function where she'd run into Luc Sanchis—literally—a year ago. Seeing her father that night had shaken her to her core, and she'd realised she needed to be a lot more prepared for when she came face to face with him.

Last week he'd had no idea that the JM in JM Holdings stood for Jesse Moriarty. She'd received an awful jolt to be reminded that she'd inherited her distinctive eye colour from him, but he hadn't recognised her and she'd hated the dart of hurt when she'd realised that.

He'd blithely launched into a spiel about how he needed a sizeable investment to stay afloat, and all the while Jesse had battled waves of sickness as she'd been hurtled back in time to when he'd stood over her, sweating, his belt marked with her blood.

She'd cut short his obsequious appeal and stood up. When he'd realised who she was he'd morphed effortlessly back into a bully and tyrant. He'd stood up too, small eyes piggy in his fleshy face, and sneered at her. 'Don't tell me this is some sort of petty revenge; did you lie awake at night dreaming of this moment?'

Jesse had flushed, because she *had*. It was the only thing that had got her through years of loneliness and bullying. The long, unending and terrifying months of grief after her mother's death. The way world around her had become a place of deep hostility, insecurity and fear, peopled by faceless social workers and harried foster carers in the grimmest parts of England.

'You're pathetic,' her father had spat out. 'Just like your mother was pathetic and naive. I should have forced her to get rid of you when I had the chance, but she begged me to let her keep you…and *this* is how you repay me?'

Jesse had focused on the deep abiding grief she felt, drawing on it for strength. 'This moment is only the culmination of my efforts to see you destroyed. No one will help you now, and when you descend into the hell of oblivion I'll be there to witness every moment of it.'

Jesse shivered a little as the distasteful memory faded. She wanted a feeling of triumph to break through the numbness but it was elusive. All she did feel, in truth, was weary. As if she'd been toiling for a long time with nothing to show for it… Yet she'd succeeded beyond her wildest dreams and she'd finally begun to realise her most personal and fervent desire…

She put down her cup and walked to the window, leaning her forehead against it, her hands on the glass either side of her shoulders. The irony of the thick glass between her and the view struck her with a sad note. Her whole life she'd felt somehow separated from everything around her.

She could picture what lay behind her all too easily: the very bare and ascetic nature of her apartment, which mirrored her personal life. Even though she'd bought it three years before, the only furniture she owned was her bed, the armchair and some kitchen furniture. She'd bought nothing because despite the wealth she'd accrued and the success she'd garnered she still didn't feel settled. She still feared her world being upended at any moment.

All she'd ever known was the certainty of inconsistency—every time she'd come to trust a social worker they'd moved on; every time she'd felt safe in a foster home she'd been moved. She'd long ago learnt to rely only on herself, trust only herself. The only constant in her life that she could depend on was her hatred of her father...

She hadn't cultivated friends or a social life. *Once* she'd been vulnerable, and there had been a man. She'd succumbed to his seduction because on some level she'd craved human contact, some tenderness. But when he'd made love to her it hadn't touched her. She'd felt like ice.

Afterwards he'd declared disgustedly, 'It's true what they say—you are like a machine.'

Jesse hadn't made the same mistake again. It had been a weakness on her part to admit to that vulnerability. Since then she'd focused on two things: her work and seeing her father brought to justice.

And now, *finally*, she was seeing the light at the end of the tunnel—a chance to let go of the past and perhaps start to *live*. She scowled. More accurately, she *had* been seeing the light at the end of the tunnel until it had been blocked by the broad shoulders of Luc Sanchis.

Jesse turned around and faced her dark and lonely-looking apartment. The thought that her father would escape defeat now, would have a chance to become successful again thanks to an investment from Luc Sanchis, was untenable. Not only that, she'd now exposed herself to her father and he would be out for her blood.

She worried at her lower lip with small teeth. She'd prepared for this day so well. Knowing how dangerous her father was, she'd investigated him thoroughly and left nothing to chance. He was rotten to the core and had avoided being put in gaol before now only because of a prodigious amount of luck, his dubious connections and his vast fortune. However, with the protection of his fortune all but gone, it was only going to be a matter of time before all his misdeeds caught up with him.

Despite her own very personal vendetta against her father, when Jesse had become aware of the corrupt extent of his greed and excess, thanks to the private investigators she'd hired, it had become about avenging much more than just her and her mother. Hers was only one tiny sad story amongst many others.

In fairness, all Jesse had had to do was to systematically attack him in a very legal and above-board way. Over the years she'd slowly but surely been buying the stocks and shares of his various concerns under the guise of different companies. She'd been weakening him from the inside out, until his foundations had grown more and more flimsy.

He'd had a lot of enemies only too happy to help that process along; she'd merely provided the push... And yet now it looked as if it had all come to naught if Luc Sanchis was going to bail him out.

Resolve made Jesse's spine tense. She couldn't give up now—not when she was so close. She had to prevent Luc Sanchis from going ahead with the deal.

She shivered slightly when she remembered the sheer physicality of the man and his presence, not to mention the power that had oozed from every cell. He would be a formidable enemy. He could break her in two if he wanted, without even batting an eyelid...but to achieve her goal she had to take that risk.

Luc was distracted and irritated. And deadly tired. He ran a hand over his face. He'd been up for almost twenty-four hours straight, making sure that his deal with O'Brien had no possible loopholes or potential hitches. The snarly London traffic wasn't helping his mood right now. At least, he thought to himself, he didn't have to worry about making his flight on time. He'd chartered a private jet to take him to his meeting in Switzerland.

He'd met with JP O'Brien the previous day and, despite

O'Brien's clear desperation, had insisted on a ten-day grace period before signing the contracts. The ten days would bring them up to the last possible date of survival for O'Brien— twenty-four hours before the banks closed in if he didn't come up with the funds. This suited Luc, as he wanted O'Brien nervous and desperate—he wanted to be O'Brien's only hope.

He smiled to himself grimly. The tiredness was worth it. He'd made sure that no one could match his offer…this time O'Brien would be *his*.

Luc found that the memory of seeing O'Brien was leading him to a much more potent memory: that of Jesse Moriarty in his office a week ago. He frowned with displeasure at finding himself thinking of her again, but her delicate features slid into his mind with annoying persistence and vividness, and his insides tightened against a frisson of awareness.

He assured himself that he was only thinking of her again because he associated her with O'Brien. There was no way she could compete with him now. If O'Brien had a counter-offer Luc would know about it. O'Brien was too desperate not to be greedy and up the stakes by playing two bidders off against each other.

Much to Luc's chagrin, his mind slid back to Jesse Moriarty like a traitor. He'd tried to get some information on her but she'd proved to be annoyingly elusive. The only details about her background were something sketchy about having been brought up in care. Maybe she was an orphan? Luc didn't like the way that thought made him remember her inherent fragility, despite her chutzpah in storming into his office the way she had and demanding answers. He had to concede that it had been a long time since anyone had had the guts to do that. And it hadn't been altogether unpleasant…

He breathed a sigh of relief when he saw that they'd left the city behind and were on the open road. The sooner he was airborne and onto his next meeting the better. It would mean welcome distraction from thinking about a pixie-sized, short-haired enigma. Just then his phone rang, and his mouth curved into a smile when he saw a familiar name.

He answered with affection, '*Cherie*…how are you today?'

What felt like a long time later, Luc became aware of waking up and feeling inordinately groggy. He opened his eyes and blinked at the bright sunlight streaming in the small window beside him. His surroundings were very quiet, but he could hear the sea in the distance and gulls overhead. The plane had obviously landed—the cabin door was open just a few feet away—but there was no sign of the air steward or pilot.

He remembered being on the phone as he'd boarded the plane, and then the flight attendant offering him coffee which he'd drunk with relish to perk up his tired mind. He'd drunk two cups, and after that remembered nothing—which was odd, because he'd intended working.

Slowly tendrils of lucidity came back into his brain, and with them finally came clarity. He looked around him. All his belongings were gone. His laptop that he'd been working on, his phone, his briefcase… He looked outside the window properly now, and the realisation hit him that he wasn't looking at the mountainous peaks of Switzerland. He was looking at an altogether hotter vista.

Feeling increasingly as if he'd stepped into a twilight zone, Luc undid his seat belt and stood up. Shaking his head free of a residual fogginess, he went to the open door and squinted into the glaring sunlight. It was *warm*. And it was most certainly not Switzerland. A faint heat haze shimmered in the distance, and the cerulean blue sky showcased the glittering waters of the… Luc blinked disbelievingly. The *Mediterranean*?

A movement out of the corner of his eye made his head swivel round, and he saw a small Jeep parked near the plane. Someone was standing by its side. It was a slim, petite figure, with short strawberry-blonde hair. Faded jeans, running shoes and a white shirt. Dark glasses hid eyes which he could recall with all too disturbing ease, despite the lingering fog in his head.

Luc slowly descended the steps attached to the plane and as the warm salt-tangy air hit him all his synapses started firing again. This was real—not a dream or the twilight zone—and he took it from the slightly defensive stance of the small woman in the distance that *she* was entirely responsible for the fact that he wasn't where he was meant to be.

Storming into his office demanding answers was one thing... This action had taken things to another level. The fact that Luc had underestimated someone for the second time in his life sent acrid anger to his gut. *No one* underestimated him any more.

He wasn't aware of the hurried movements behind him when his feet touched the tarmac, but as soon as he walked away from the steps the air steward appeared in the plane's doorway to haul the steps back up out of sight, and the door was closed. Luc went towards Jesse Moriarty and came to a stop just feet away, head thrown back, nostrils flaring, and he stared down at her from his considerable height advantage.

'Well, well, Ms Moriarty, fancy meeting you here. Are you going to tell me where I am?' His voice dripped with ice.

He could see Jesse's slim throat work as she swallowed. The fact that she wasn't as cool as she was obviously striving to appear did nothing for his temper levels.

Slowly she supplied, 'Greece. This is a privately owned Greek island, which I'm renting.'

'That's nice. And you felt compelled to bring me along to join you on your holiday?'

Jesse didn't answer immediately and Luc added caustically, 'If I'd known how desperate you were for my company we could have come to some arrangement.'

He could see her cheeks flush red and she bit out, 'It's not…not like that. That's not why you're here.'

Somehow that had a more incendiary effect on Luc than finding himself landed in a different country from the one he'd been flying to. He closed the distance between them and grabbed Jesse's arms in two hands, shaking her. She was so slight that her sunglasses fell off with the motion, revealing those huge grey eyes, stormy with swirling emotions, staring up at him.

'Well? Are you going to tell me what the hell I'm doing here?'

'I…' She gulped visibly, and then said more forcibly, 'I've kidnapped you.'

# CHAPTER THREE

Luc Sanchis's hands were painfully tight on her arms, but Jesse wouldn't emit so much as a squeak to let him know. She looked up into those flashing dark brown eyes and noticed for the first time that he had the most absurdly long lashes. She blinked. This was crazy! She'd just kidnapped one of the world's most influential men and she was noticing his *eyelashes*?

Jerkily, and with a lot of effort, Jesse pulled free of Luc Sanchis's tight grip; she knew she'd be bruised. He was still staring at her, stunned. Fear pierced Jesse for a second. He looked okay, but what if he'd been allergic to—?

Suddenly his slightly stunned look changed to something much cooler and *angry*. 'I presume you had them slip something into my coffee?'

Jesse flushed. She could see the small plane now almost at the other end of the runway out of the corner of her eye. Neither of them had even noticed the low throb of the engine.

'I asked them to put a herbal sleeping aid into your coffee. I was hoping it would make you too groggy to notice the detour in your flight, and also give them time to take your things. We didn't know it would knock you out.'

Grimly Luc surmised that that was because they hadn't known how tired he was. He wasn't feeling any lingering effects of the herbal remedy now, so he knew it hadn't been anything stronger.

He heard the throttle of the plane roar behind him as it geared up to make its dash back down the runway. Luc turned around and saw it start its run, gathering speed. As he watched it come closer and closer and faster incredulity kept him immobile. He realised that this was the first time in a long time that things had deviated off the tracks of his well-ordered life, and along with the incredulity was something much more ambiguous.

The small plane sped past him, bringing a small tornado of wind and hot air in its wake, and he watched with a hand over his eyes as it lifted up into the clear blue sky and banked to the right, with the sunlight glinting mockingly off its black wings.

That fleeting feeling of something ambiguous dissolved as the enormity of what had happened hit Luc. He looked down at Jesse Moriarty now, his insides tensing at the reality of how petite she was—especially in flat shoes. Her short hair had been whipped up by the wind, leaving it tousled and surprisingly sexy against her delicate skull. Then he remembered her arrogance in his office last week—her proposal to match his buy-out. Luc crossed his arms and felt the acrid burn of anger in his gut.

Jesse gulped; she had seen the way Luc Sanchis's disbelieving eyes had followed the plane's ascent. He was looking down at *her* now, though, and his eyes were flat and hard. Completely emotionless. Jesse knew that along with her father she'd just made possibly the worst enemy of her life.

As the noise of the plane became fainter and fainter silence surrounded them again, only broken by the sound of small chirruping insects in the distance, stopping and starting.

Luc Sanchis's voice was silky when it came, disconcerting and jarring.

'You do know that you're looking at possibly eight years' imprisonment for this stunt?'

Jesse nodded slowly. She'd had to weigh up all the possible consequences, but the main one would be that her father wouldn't be bailed out by Luc Sanchis—and that was all that mattered.

'I know what I'm doing,' she said now, as much to herself as to Luc Sanchis.

His face was tight, the lines starkly beautiful against the blue sky. 'Where are my things—my laptop, phone...*passport*?'

Jesse fought not to quail under his censorious gaze and tone. She swallowed. 'They're in a safe place...and will be given back to you on the day you leave.'

The sound of tension was evident in his voice. 'And when will that be?'

Jesse felt the tightness in her chest. 'When the deadline has come and gone on your deal with O'Brien.'

When it would be too late to make sure that he had O'Brien where he wanted him.

Luc reeled, and his mind almost closed down at that unpalatable prospect. Fury gripped him like a physical force. To be rendered so powerless, helpless... For the first time in his life he felt capable of violence.

He stepped back. He forced air into his lungs and shook his head. 'Unbelievable... You want him this badly yourself?'

Jesse felt hard inside. No one else had come forward to save O'Brien, and if she could hold Sanchis off until it was too late her father would effectively be a sinking ship that no one would touch. He'd be mired in legal red tape for years, and Jesse knew that once people started looking into his affairs his years of tax evasion, corruption and fraud would catch up with him. He'd most certainly be facing a gaol sentence.

Luc Sanchis wouldn't touch him then, for fear of being embroiled in his mess. Everything she'd learned about his pristine ethics and business practices told Jesse that. In a way, if he'd turned out to be as corrupt as her father it would have made this easier...

'Yes,' Jesse said firmly, 'I want him this badly.'

Luc Sanchis stepped closer again, and Jesse couldn't help a small faltering step backwards, hating herself for showing him the slightest weakness.

'You've made a very grave error in deciding to fight me on this matter.'

Jesse forced steel into her spine and looked straight into those dark eyes. 'I offered you an opportunity to step aside and you didn't take it.'

Luc Sanchis stepped even closer, intimidating, his scent woodsy and distracting.

'All you've done here is make yourself a foe for life. When I'm done with you, you'll be lucky to get work in an internet café.'

Luc welcomed the rage simmering inside him. It was distracting him from how delicate Jesse Moriarty appeared even when she'd just kidnapped him! He'd spent so long dreaming of the moment when he'd have O'Brien exactly where he wanted him, and now he was looking at years of plans gone to waste.

He had to step away from Moriarty and her *faux* vulnerability and turn around. Spiking his hands in his hair, his muscles bunched with angry tension, Luc wanted to smash his fist into something solid. Preferably a wall. But nothing surrounded him except the mocking silence of this mystery island.

He whirled round again, taking in her pale features. That angered him even more. 'Where the hell *are* we? And *don't* just say "a Greek island" again.'

Jesse bit her lip so hard she could feel blood. When Luc

Sanchis had turned away from her just now she'd had a very real sense that he wanted to hit something.

She quickly considered his question and decided that there was nothing he could do about it anyway. 'We are on a small uninhabited island called Oxakis. It's privately owned. It's one of the most remote islands in the Greek archipelago.'

Sanchis bit back a curse. Out of the thousands of islands and islets in Greece he knew only a few hundred were inhabited. They could literally be anywhere right now, and there was no land in sight. And nothing that signified any other kind of habitation on this island.

'That's handy, then, isn't it?'

It was rather, Jesse thought a little hysterically. As was the fact that the very security-conscious owner had made his sumptuous villa—the only dwelling on the island—practically impregnable once you were within the alarmed fence... which was where she needed to get Luc Sanchis now, so she could be assured of his location at all times.

More jerkily than she liked, Jesse moved back towards the Jeep and the driver's side. Luc Sanchis just stood there, staring at her. Jesse's conscience struck her hard and she had to force down the feeling. From what she'd read about him, this man was one of the least vulnerable on the planet.

She'd unearthed the infamous story of how he'd wreaked revenge on an ex-lover who had betrayed him by decimating her reputation so comprehensively that the woman had suffered a very public nervous breakdown. It had sent out a clear message to anyone who thought they could play Luc Sanchis: *they couldn't.*

And yet here *she* was, doing exactly that.

When he didn't immediately follow her to the Jeep, panic struck Jesse. She was no match physically for this man, and at that thought an insidious burn began in her belly, the effortless awareness she seemed to have around him intensifying.

She bit out, more caustically than she'd intended, 'There's nothing else on the island except the villa. You can stay here if you want, but it'll be a long wait and it gets cold at night.' She added, 'We're not under a flight path, and no boats or ships sail close to this island.'

Jesse could see his hands clench into fists. He should have looked incongruous against this backdrop, in his dark suit, shirt and tie, but he seemed to meld with the harsh rock formations in the distance. And the searing sunlight only made his olive skin seem more exotic. He'd run his hands through his hair and it was slightly tousled, giving him a devilish air.

That angry tension was practically vibrating off him now, but after a tense inner struggle that Jesse could practically *feel* he bit out, 'Damn you, Moriarty.'

He ripped off his jacket, taking it in one hand, and with his other hand reached up to undo the top button of his shirt under the tie. He strode towards the passenger side of the Jeep and almost pulled the door off its hinges. It visibly sagged under his weight when he got in and sat down.

Wiping suddenly sweaty hands on her jeans, Jesse picked up her fallen sunglasses and opened her own door and got in too, hoping he wouldn't notice the tremor in her hand as she put the key in the ignition. The engine fired to life. When she pressed on the accelerator too hard and they jerked forward her cheeks burned under his scathing look, which she could feel like a brand on her skin.

Taking a deep breath, Jesse navigated the Jeep out of the airfield and onto the one very narrow road which led around to the other side of the island and the villa.

Luc's hand was clenched tight around the handle above the door. The Jeep felt like a prison cell—compounded by the fact that *he* wasn't in the driving seat. He *hated* not driving unless he was in the back of his chauffeur-driven car. He winced as Jesse changed gear and they screeched. The Jeep was new and luxurious, but his long legs were still cramped. He was uncomfortably aware of how stretched out *her* legs had to be to reach the pedals.

She was like a doll. He imagined that he could wrap one hand all the way around one taut jean-clad thigh. Her hands were tiny on the steering wheel. The sleeves of her shirt were rolled up, revealing slim arms and slender wrists.

Luc felt himself turning so he could scrutinise her even closer, almost unaware of what he was doing. The top button of her shirt was open, revealing pale skin at the bottom of her throat and long neck. The seat belt cut across her chest, making the small swells of her breasts appear more prominent.

Suddenly her head turned and she cast him a quick suspicious glance. 'What are you looking at?'

With more effort than he cared to admit he dragged his gaze up to see pink cheeks and those long-lashed dark grey eyes. He noticed that her lips were soft and surprisingly full—especially the bottom lip. Luc felt very peculiar for a fleeting moment, and then cursed himself and swung back to face the road.

'A way out,' he muttered acerbically, telling himself that this awareness of her was a pure side effect of the extraordinary circumstances. He could feel the shock wearing off, and suddenly thought of something.

He looked back at her grim profile and tried not to notice her stubborn chin or the straight line of her nose. Crossing his arms across his chest, he sat back against the door and regarded her. 'I'm expected in Switzerland for a meeting at the economic forum; people will already be wondering where I am and asking questions. My security staff on the ground there will be mounting a search as soon as I don't arrive.'

Jesse's hands tightened on the steering wheel. She could see the huge wrought-iron gates of the villa up ahead and breathed a sigh of relief. She really didn't want to have the next part of this conversation in a confined space when she needed all her concentration. Her driving wasn't assured at the best of times.

She ignored Luc Sanchis and once they were through the gates pressed a button in the Jeep which activated their closure behind them. Finally she felt a little bit more secure.

The driveway was a steep climb up to the villa, which rested on a high rocky outcrop overlooking the sea. On either side a wall of lush bougainvillaea bushes with pink and purple flowers lined the route.

She saw out of the corner of her eye that Luc Sanchis had glanced back too, to see the gates close, and felt a fresh wave of enmity coming from him.

The villa that came into view was a stunning example of the old style—nothing jarring or modern. The classic, elegant lines of the two-storey house drew the eye down to floor level, with three long French windows and a patio. Wooden shutters were painted a faint eggshell, offset by walls painted a warm cream colour. Traditional terracotta tiles on the roof were faded from the sunlight. Trees and bushes slightly obscured the steps leading up to a green lawn, which led to the patio outside the French doors.

Gravel crunched under the wheels of the Jeep as Jesse bypassed the steps up to the patio and drove to the main door. A glorious profusion of flowers bloomed everywhere from pots and trellises. But Jesse was blind to the magical beauty of the place.

She brought the Jeep to a stop outside the main door and cut the engine.

Sarcastically Luc Sanchis asked, 'No butler to greet us and open the door?'

Jesse was so tense she felt as if she might snap. 'There are no staff. Just us.' She got out quickly, before Luc Sanchis's blistering anger and energy could make her feel even more claustrophobic.

He got out too, and faced her across the bonnet of the Jeep. Jesse pressed the button to lock the Jeep and carefully pocketed the keys. Luc Sanchis's eyes tracked her movements. And then he looked back up.

'Well? You haven't answered my question. What are you going to do when my security team locate the GPS signal on my mobile phone and track me to here?' He glanced at the heavy platinum watch encircling one broad wrist. 'I'd say all hell is breaking loose right about now…'

Jesse sent up a sigh of relief that she'd had enough time to store his personal effects in a locked security box which was now locked inside the boot of the Jeep.

She hitched up her chin and faced him. 'I disabled the GPS device on your phone *and* laptop. There's no other way your location can be centred to here.' She could see his jaw clench ominously and rushed on. 'And I hacked into your account to send e-mails to your assistant and your security team, to alert them to a change of plan in your schedule. I said that you were not to be disturbed under any circumstances until you contacted them.'

Jesse could see his brain clicking into gear…sorting through what she'd said…searching for a way out. Then she saw realisation hit, and he stalked around the front of the Jeep, seriously intimidating now.

'You're one of the only people in the world who could do such a thing because you devised the software.'

Jesse gulped. She might have felt proud in other circumstances, but not right now, when she said, 'Yes.'

If he hadn't already gone nuclear this just might have done it.

Jesse spoke again—as much to distract him as anything else. 'I'm aware that you are known for abrupt changes in plan—as much to keep your employees on their toes as to keep an eye on your myriad business interests—so I don't think your staff will be too surprised at your sudden deviation.'

Jesse could see how his cheeks suffused with colour, making his cheekbones stand out even further, only adding to his intensely masculine appeal. His voice was supremely controlled when he spoke, but it wasn't fooling Jesse for a second. She could see a muscle twitching in his hard jaw.

'You certainly seem to have thought of everything. For now.'

'For the next ten days, Mr Sanchis. I've…*you've* already sent out instructions to back out of the deal with O'Brien.'

'Kidnapping; hacking into my accounts; pretending to be me… Your crimes are mounting, Ms Moriarty. And all because you're so desperate to be the one to save O'Brien from the abyss.'

*No!* Jesse wanted to scream. *I want to be the one to send him into the abyss. For ever!*

She lifted one shoulder in a small movement, scared of that flat, emotionless look in Luc Sanchis's eyes. With his tie rakishly askew and his shirt open he might have been a pirate. He spat out words contemptuously, taking Jesse by surprise.

'Women like you make me sick. You're more ruthless than any man. In light of your determination to succeed in this matter I don't doubt you'd buy and sell a family member to get what you want.'

Jesse was unaware of how she paled in that instant, or of how Luc Sanchis's eyes narrowed on her. She stepped back abruptly avoiding his eyes, more than aghast at how easily he'd cut her to the quick. It was because of treacherous family that she was in this position. That she even knew what ruthlessness felt like.

'Let me show you around the villa.'

Tension quivered between them, and Jesse knew that Luc Sanchis was realising he simply had no option right now except to do as she said. She walked around him and up some steps into the main hall.

The house throughout was white, with exposed stone walls, bright and comfortable furnishings. The main hall floor was marble, but the rest of the ground level had wooden floors, softened by faded oriental rugs. It was truly a home, loved and tended by its owners—a Greek billionaire named Alexandros Kouros, his wife, Kallie, and their three children.

Jesse had done some business with Kouros in the past, and he'd told her about his island and villa and suggested that she use it if she ever felt like getting away, if it was free. She'd automatically said thanks but no thanks; leisure was not something she indulged in.

She'd remembered the island when she'd thought of this audacious plan to stop Luc Sanchis, and had wondered where on earth she could take him.

She gestured to the vast expanse of a plush living room, with floor-to-ceiling bookshelves along one wall and comfortable couches and chairs. 'This is the main living area. There's a TV and DVDs in the cabinet…'

His voice dripped sarcasm. 'You mean I'm allowed to move freely throughout the house? You're not locking me in the tower with only a daily bowl of gruel to keep me alive?'

Jesse tensed at his dark humour. She was surprised…she'd not been sure what to expect. In her experience billionaires and titans of industry could be petulant when things didn't go their way. And Luc Sanchis so far had barely balked at his fate…he was very angry, yes, but not disconcerted. As if he was merely biding his time, getting the lie of the land.

She didn't fool herself into believing she could be complacent. Luc Sanchis was preternaturally intelligent and cunning. She wouldn't trust for a second that he wasn't looking for a way out, or a way to manipulate her.

She turned around to face him, struck all over again at his immense physicality. She didn't like how it made her feel weak. He had to understand how futile any attempt on his part to leave would be.

'There is a perimeter fence around this villa that is permanently electrified and alarmed with infra-red sensors. That airstrip is the only way on and off the island.'

Jesse crossed her fingers behind her back, because she knew there was a small boathouse tucked away on the southern tip which held a speedboat. She didn't like the way Luc Sanchis's eyes narrowed on her contemplatively.

He crossed his arms, legs spread. Supremely comfortable in his skin even now. 'I'm a champion swimmer.'

*Why am I not surprised?* Jesse thought caustically.

She crossed her arms too. 'The waters here are treacherous, known for their volatile currents. I checked the weather forecast and a storm is possible. Even if you did make it through the perimeter fence, no matter how good a swimmer you are you'd never last.'

Luc cast a glance through the open French doors and the gently billowing white curtains. The scene outside was idyllic, but even as he thought that the faintest whisper of a cool breeze whistled through the room. He knew only too well from his experience as a seasoned sailor how the weather could change in an instant.

He looked back down into those serious grey eyes and had a fleeting thought: *why so serious?*

He shook his head, as if that would obliterate the insidious question. 'How did you persuade my pilot to change course?' He had been wondering about that. He had still been on the phone when he'd embarked on the plane, right up until they'd been about to take off. Undoubtedly that had added to the ease with which they'd carried out their subterfuge.

Jesse avoided his eye again, looking down for a moment, blushing furiously. 'I...ah...sent his company an e-mail too. From you...explaining that you wanted to change your flight plan from Switzerland to here. And that you didn't want to discuss it once you got on board...because the trip was of a romantic nature.'

She looked back up. 'I contracted the steward separately and paid him to administer the sleeping aid, and he took your things as well,' she admitted. 'It was all done under the impression that it wasn't serious but for a *romantic*...' Jesse's voice trailed off with embarrassment, but then she got herself together. 'I also said that you'd inform them when you wanted to book your return flight.'

Luc gritted his jaw so tightly it hurt. She'd simply but effectively re-routed his entire schedule—and with the best anti-hacking software protecting his systems who would assume for a second the messages weren't coming from him? He was hoist by his own petard because, exactly as she'd pointed out, his staff *were* used to his last-minute changes. She'd obviously sent all these missives at the last possible moment, and worded them in such a way that they didn't encourage discussion. Something he was apt to do when he wanted to focus on something.

Jesse had no idea what was going on in his head now, but she was sure it wasn't pretty and had a lot to do with hating her. She backed away towards the stairs, which led up to the upper rooms and away from the living space. After a few taut seconds she heard Luc Sanchis sigh and come after her.

A carpeted runner led up the stairs to a corridor on the first level that had rooms leading off in each direction. Jesse stopped outside one and opened the door, standing aside so Sanchis could look inside.

She'd felt funny about using the Kouroses' master bedroom, so she'd picked the next largest for Luc Sanchis and taken a modest one for herself, instinctively feeling more comfortable in less opulent surroundings. Although, she thought wryly, *modest* in this villa meant a palatial bedroom with plush carpets and a queen-sized bed. Her huge *en suite* bathroom had a decadent sunken bath, and led out to a balcony with a stunning view of the Mediterranean Sea.

She walked into the bedroom she'd assigned for Luc Sanchis, her feet sinking noiselessly into the carpet. The view from this room and its *en suite* bathroom were even more spectacular than that from Jesse's room.

She was cursory when she spoke, suddenly uncomfortable here with this man in such luxurious surroundings. 'This is the main bedroom with *en suite* bathroom. It's stocked with all the necessary toiletries.'

Jesse fought not to flinch when Luc Sanchis joined her in the bathroom and inspected the shelves, picking things up and putting them down again. She noticed that he must have dropped his jacket and tie somewhere. A minute ago the rooms had felt enormous. Now Jesse felt positively claustrophobic. All she could see were those big hands and long fingers making everything look tiny.

She backed out into the bedroom and noticed the jacket and tie strewn on the bed. She looked away hurriedly, suddenly hot when she thought of him ripping that tie off.

She walked over to the doors leading into a walk-in closet. She could sense Luc Sanchis and his bristling energy close behind her, and hated the little shiver of *something* she felt inside.

With the doors open wide she indicated to where a vast array of clothes was laid out. Suits, trousers, shoes. Casual clothes, pyjamas. Luc Sanchis stepped up to the door and his mouth opened…and closed again. Eyes flashing he looked at Jesse and muttered grimly, 'I suspected you might be gay, but not if these belong to the last gigolo you brought here.'

Jesse's face flamed and she fought for control. He thought these were for her *lovers*? The idea would have been laughable if Jesse had been in the mood to laugh. And she was stung somewhere very vulnerable to think that he'd assumed she was gay.

Luc watched Jesse. Myriad expressions chased across her face—uppermost something looking like shock. He was surprised at this prudish aspect of her but then recalled the buttoned-up look she'd sported in his office. She was more casual now, but equally unrevealing. He didn't like to admit to the stab of something incomprehensible in his gut when he thought of these clothes belonging to another man.

She got out in a slightly strangled-sounding voice, 'They're all new. For you. I knew your meeting was only for a couple of hours and you wouldn't have clothes with you…so I ordered some.'

Luc walked into the space and fingered some of the clothes. There was enough to dress him for a month, encompassing the entire spectrum of casual to formal wear.

Jesse said hesitantly from behind him, 'Mr Sanchis, I know I've brought you here against your will, but it really is my intention to let you go…just as soon as I'm assured you won't be in a position to resurrect your deal with O'Brien…'

Sounding more hopeful than he'd ever heard her, she went on, 'If you could tell me now that you're willing to sign a contract stating that you'll walk away from the deal then I can have a plane or a helicopter here within the hour.'

Luc held the material of a black tuxedo jacket between thumb and forefinger. He stopped himself from gripping the material in his fist and squeezing with all the strength in his body. He looked at her.

'No way.'

And then he dismissed her by looking back to the clothes. Most disturbingly, they were all in his exact size.

'Don't tell me—you hacked into my assistant's brief on what to order from my tailor?'

Luc could hear Jesse shift uncomfortably.

'The information was easy to find. I wanted to make sure you'd be as comfortable as possible, Mr Sanchis.'

Luc dropped the jacket and stalked towards Jesse. He placed an arm above her head against the doorframe and saw how her eyes widened. Her cheeks flushed and her breathing grew more rapid. *Interesting*. Much to his chagrin, his own breathing felt a tiny bit more laboured.

Disgusted with himself, Luc dropped his arm and said curtly, 'I think we've skipped enough levels of social niceties to earn first-name status don't you? Luc is my name.'

Jesse felt as if she was floundering badly. When he'd stalked over to her just now she'd felt a drowning sensation. Her insides had tightened while simultaneously feeling as if they were melting. And her nipples were as hard as bullets against the lace of her bra.

Before she could react he was stalking away from her and out of the room. Jesse started after him, calling, 'Where are you going?'

He said, without turning around, 'To find a phone so I can call someone and arrange to get off this godforsaken island and away from *you*. This ridiculous charade has gone on long enough.'

He stopped abruptly at the bottom of the stairs and Jesse almost careened into his back. She stopped herself just in time. He was looking from left to right and then he strode off, opening and closing doors to various rooms. Jesse's heart was thumping, and she held her breath when he came to the door of the study. He opened it and went in, and she winced when she heard a very crude curse.

He came back out, hands on hips, expression thunderous. 'You've removed any means of internet communication—I take it the landline too?'

Jesse nodded slowly. She'd locked everything securely into the villa's safe. She had her own phone, of course, but that was safely tucked away where Sanchis couldn't find it.

He came close to Jesse and she fought to hold her ground— even when he came so close that all she could smell was his scent and she had to tip her head back to look at him.

'You *will* pay for this, Jesse…you know that, don't you? I'll do whatever it takes to get off this island.'

# CHAPTER FOUR

THE threat in Luc's voice was explicit, but disturbingly all Jesse felt was a coil of tension low down in her belly at hearing him use her name for the first time. It made her want to squirm.

She refused to acknowledge that physical reaction, or let him intimidate her, and said, 'I know that my actions will have consequences, and I don't care.'

Because all she did care about was making sure that her father faced up to the consequences of *his* actions and was rendered impotent. Finally.

Luc looked so deeply into Jesse's eyes for such a long moment that she literally started to feel dizzy, and then finally he stepped back. She breathed out. Abruptly he turned and started to stalk away from her, clearly looking for something else. After a moment Jesse hurried after him again.

She found him in the kitchen at the back of the villa, which had French doors opening out onto a terraced area and a lush garden, where a pool and pool house were tucked away behind artful foliage. It was stupendously idyllic, but unfortunately completely wasted on Jesse and her very reluctant guest.

Luc was opening and closing doors and cupboards. He acknowledged her presence without turning around. 'There's enough food here for an army.'

Weakly, because she couldn't seem to take her eyes off the

way his trousers were stretched across hard buttocks, Jesse said, 'It's enough to last about two weeks, actually.'

He straightened up and turned around and Jesse averted her gaze upwards guiltily.

Luc placed his hands on the island in the centre of the kitchen. 'Two weeks?'

Jesse swallowed. 'Just in case of any unforeseen eventualities.'

'What kind of *eventualities*, Jesse?'

Jesse's insides felt funny again at hearing him say her name. In a rush she said, 'Like a storm, or something out of our control, extending our stay longer than I'd planned.'

Luc turned away again with a muttered curse. He started taking things out of the fridge and cupboards, laying them out on the counter.

A little redundantly Jesse asked, 'What are you doing?'

'Making myself something to eat—as if it wasn't glaringly obvious.'

His sarcasm bounced off Jesse. She was more than surprised to see how dextrous he was at whipping up a delicious-looking sandwich in minutes. He pulled a bottle of water from the fridge, and then after a second reached in again and took out a chilled bottle of wine. With an economy of movement he pulled the cork from the bottle with a corkscrew, and then put the water under his arm and the wine and sandwich in respective hands.

He completely ignored Jesse and made his way back out of the kitchen and up the stairs to the bedrooms.

Jesse followed him and asked, 'Where are you going?'

Luc stopped at the top of the stairs and sighed. He turned around. 'I'm going to my room to eat and drink and get away from *you*—which seems to be about the only thing I *can* do at the moment.'

Jesse saw one very large hand clamped around the wine bottle and her throat felt dry. 'Don't you need a glass?'

'No,' came the curt reply, 'I don't need a glass.'

And with that he turned and disappeared. A couple of seconds later she winced as she heard the slamming of a door.

Jesse turned around and sank down onto the bottom stair. The enormity of everything that had happened hit her then, and she lifted a hand to her head. It was trembling from the adrenalin. The main front door was still open, and she looked out blankly at the benignly beautiful view.

She had managed to incarcerate Luc Sanchis on this island. She was now alone, for the next ten days at least, with one of the world's most powerful men and a potentially lethal enemy. She recalled how he'd turned on the stairs, his entire body moving with innately masculine grace, and heat pooled in her lower belly. He was six feet four of hard, muscle-packed, angry testosterone, and the look in his eyes just now had been murderous.

Luc sat in a chair on his private balcony. The Mediterranean stretched out as far as the eye could see, with not another piece of land or a boat in sight. The threat of a storm appeared to have passed for the moment and the glorious view mocked him. His hand was still wrapped around the neck of the wine bottle and he lifted it to his mouth and took another healthy slug, noting that he'd managed to demolish half of it already.

Disgusted, because he was usually more than abstemious when it came to alcohol, he slammed it down on the table beside him, alongside the half-eaten sandwich. He'd taken the wine from the fridge on a whim and had relished Jesse's wide-eyed response to him pulling it out.

Damn her anyway, this pixie-sized, short-haired witch.

He still couldn't quite believe what she'd managed to do to him—and with such ease. That perhaps was worst of all, when he thought of it. How he'd happily walked right into her trap. The modern-day communications that everyone took so much for granted had allowed her to rearrange his schedule with no questions asked. He grimaced. It was all thanks to the fact that she was effectively a computer nerd. Although when he pictured a nerd he saw a twenty-year-old weedy guy in glasses. Not a petite and annoyingly vulnerable-looking blonde-haired elf. He snorted. *Vulnerable?* As if.

Luc grabbed the wine bottle again almost rebelliously; the more wine he drank, the more her image in his head grew blurry, so he took another gulp.

He sat forward with the bottle dangling from his fingers, completely unaware of the rakish image he presented, with his shirt buttons ripped apart, exposing the top of his chest.

He could almost laugh. But it wasn't funny in the slightest. Only last week his secretary had enquired solicitously as to whether he'd thought about scheduling any holiday time for the rest of the year. She'd probably be assuming right now that he'd taken her concern as advice. And he knew she wouldn't question his *apparent* change of direction when it came to the O'Brien deal, because she was used to him changing his mind and not explaining why. It rankled bitterly now. He didn't know Jesse Moriarty from Adam and yet she seemed to have read him like a book.

And the two people in the world who cared about him most were currently at sea on a two-week cruise. Only this morning he'd told his mother and sister with affectionate mock severity that he didn't want to hear from them unless there was a serious life-or-death crisis.

He smiled mirthlessly at the irony. In normal circumstances his mother started panicking if she didn't get her habitual daily phone call—even though she'd become much more relaxed since marrying her second husband, George, the previous year.

For the first time since Luc could remember his mother and sister didn't *need* him in quite the same all-encompassing way, and he wasn't sure how comfortable he was with that. Responsibility for them was so ingrained in him that it had pervaded outwards to every facet of his life, influencing every decision because what he did affected them.

Ever since his father had died when he was twelve, he'd been inured with a hyper-awareness of his duty. He could still remember the way people had looked at him sadly at his father's funeral and told him that he was the man of the family now.

Coupled with that later betrayal, which had cemented cynical distrust onto his psyche, Luc had become accustomed to being surprised by little. But he *was* surprised now. And he was angry. Because Jesse Moriarty was thwarting long-cherished plans to—

Luc heard a sound and the cacophony of thoughts in his head stopped abruptly. It had come from below him, out on the terrace which led down to the idyllic pool just visible through the trees.

He rested the wine bottle on the ground beside him and stood up, putting his hands on the railing surrounding his balcony. And then he saw her, walking onto the grass and down towards the trees.

She was wearing a short robe, and his eyes were drawn to slender but shapely pale legs. She carried a towel in one hand and disappeared into the trees. Her purpose became apparent when Luc heard the faint sound of a splash, and he could just make out the movement of arms scissoring in and out of the water through the greenery.

His hands curled tight around the railing and a coil of tension came into his belly. With a growl of disgust, because he found himself wondering if she was wearing a bikini or a one-piece, and how she might fill it out with that petite, lithe form, Luc turned back into his room, away from the view.

He paced back and forth, anger rising in him like a tide at witnessing her acting so unaffected—taking a nonchalant swim as if she *hadn't* just kidnapped him! What the hell was he doing, wondering what she was wearing, when he didn't even find her attractive? He ignored the betraying heat in his blood that contradicted him.

He recalled the way her face had tightened and she'd shut down in his office when he'd asked her about her reasons for wanting to save O'Brien. Clearly conversation wasn't going to be an option now, if she hadn't revealed her reasons then.

*Think, man, think,* he remonstrated with himself, cursing the mild fog of wine now. So far she'd executed his kidnap with the minimum of fuss and fanfare. It had been utterly simple but so effective—which made it galling. Luc would have almost preferred it if he'd been hit over the back of the head and knocked unconscious. At least that way he'd feel less culpable…

He shook his head. He had to deal with the fact that he was here now, and he needed to get off this island as soon as possible.

His mind skipped over everything and kept returning a big fat blank. He could overpower her easily, of course, but Luc's insides recoiled at that scenario. And what would that serve? She obviously had some means of communication with the outside world, but he didn't doubt that it would be well hidden—and that could be anywhere in this vast villa. And he had the sneaking suspicion that even if he did find whatever device she had it would be password-protected and impossible for him to break into.

She hadn't seemed intimidated by the fact that she could go to gaol for this, and when he'd threatened her with ruination it had brokered a very blasé response. Clearly being the one to secure JP O'Brien's survival was far more important to her than anything he could threaten her with…and that thought made bile rise from his gut.

Luc realised that he couldn't hear the sound of water splashing any more and paced back to the balcony. The light was falling now, and dusk was bathing the island in a mauve glow. Jesse suddenly appeared from the trees, rubbing her hair with a towel, once again in that short robe. Luc instinctively ducked back into the shadows, but as if she sensed his eyes on her her head came up sharply, and she looked up in the direction of his room.

Luc saw the tension in her frame, in the way her hand tightened on the towel. Her hair was sticking up in little tufts on her head, and he had the sudden urge to curl his hand around the delicate stem of her neck and…*throttle her*, he told himself angrily, watching as she ducked her head and hurried out of view again.

He cursed himself volubly and denied with every breath in his body that for a moment he'd wanted to be standing in front of her, so he could bring her head closer and tip it up so that he could taste just how soft her lips were.

Luc went into the bathroom and turned on the shower. He stripped and stood under the pounding spray. With fists clenched he placed his hands on the tiled walls, his whole body taut with anger, tension…and something much more insidious.

He had no option but to ensure he got off this island before the ten days were up, and he would do whatever it took to achieve that outcome. But, short of torturing Jesse Moriarty to force her to hand over her phone or to communicate with the outside world for him, Luc couldn't see a solution.

And then it came to him—sneaking into his consciousness with a wicked wink. He'd seen the tiny telltale physical response Jesse had shown to his proximity earlier. It could have been just nerves…or it could have been something else.

A form of torture might not be so beyond the realms of possibility after all—but this would be a very *sensual* form of torture. Designed to sneak past every prickly defence he'd seen so far and uncover the beating heart of the woman, and in so doing render her completely helpless to him.

Jesse was sitting in a chair at the kitchen table, having just eaten a bowl of cereal. The Kouros housekeeper had left the fridge and larder stocked to the gills, *enough for an army*, as Luc had said.

Jesse grimaced; unfortunately it would appear that the housekeeper had expected gourmands, because nothing was ready-made and she cursed that oversight now.

Jesse had to admit that unless Luc Sanchis displayed a skill for making something more complicated than a sandwich they might well starve. She couldn't boil an egg without burning both it and the water.

She was coiled tighter than a spring, waiting for some sign of Luc Sanchis, figuring he'd have to eat again at some stage. He was a big man, and unlikely to find enough nourishment in a sandwich. But to her knowledge he was still in his room and hadn't left it since he'd gone there earlier.

Hating how on edge she was, she got up to wash her things in the sink. From where she stood she could see out to where the pool house was just visible through the trees, gleaming whitely in the dusk. The calming effect of her swim earlier had lasted only until she'd looked up to Luc Sanchis's balcony, because she'd thought she'd seen a movement, but it had only been the gently billowing curtain. Nevertheless his image had been immediate in her mind's eye. His tall and well-built frame. Those dark, angry eyes.

She'd hurried back into the villa and straight to her room,

where she'd dressed in her habitual casual uniform of jeans and a loose top. Usually she was barely aware of the clothes she wore, but as she'd pulled on the jeans she'd felt an alien sense of yearning for something *softer*.

She reflected to herself that she'd never consciously set out to favour less feminine apparel, but the fact was she didn't own anything remotely *soft*, and not even one dress.

She looked at other women sometimes and something very secret inside her envied their easy femininity—the way they revelled in it and celebrated it. Hers had been locked away for so long now that she didn't know if she could ever explore it again.

Her one concession to her hidden femininity was her love of opulent perfumes. The more heady and sensual the better...

Luc's caustic comment that she might be gay mocked her. Some of Jesse's closest colleagues were gay, and in truth she envied them their confidence and freedom of expression, even if she didn't share their preferences.

She put down the dishcloth and absently touched her short hair, which she could see reflected more clearly in the window as it got darker outside. Inexplicably she thought of something she hadn't remembered in years: her first foster mother and her scathing voice.

*'Nits. Disgusting thing you're bringing into my house. Your hair is far too long as it is. Don't know how it hasn't been cut before now. You're just lucky I worked in a hairdresser's, my girl. We'll soon have the lot off and those little buggers gone...'*

The woman had been oblivious to Jesse's tears as her almost waist length fair locks had fallen away to the floor. Jesse's mother had had the same glorious hair, and since she'd died Jesse had got used to sleeping at night with a skein of her own hair wrapped around her hand. It had given her a comforting sense that her mother was still there.

The same foster parent had given the few dresses Jesse had owned to her own daughter, who'd been a little younger, declaring, *'You won't be needing those any more...'* But she hadn't minded so much about the dresses. They had come from her father—leftovers of the few occasions when he had displayed anything remotely resembling patriarchal awareness. He would arrive and bestow some lavishly decorated box on Jesse before telling her to clear off while he locked himself and her mother into her mother's bedroom.

Since that day in the foster home when she'd been so brutally shorn she'd never let her hair grow long. She'd felt so nakedly vulnerable that day that she'd vowed never to let anyone be able to do such a thing to her again...and she'd controlled that by insisting on regular haircuts, sometimes cutting it herself if she had to.

Jesse tried to rationalise that perhaps she was in this strange reflective mood now because of the day's stressful events, but she realised that she didn't have to fear such a scenario ever again. Of course she'd known that for a long time, but keeping her hair short had become a deeply ingrained habit. A kind of armour.

A very fleeting thrill of excitement surged in her belly at the thought that she could possibly let her hair grow...and then she caught the wistful expression on her own face and grimaced at her reflection before turning back into the kitchen—only to come face to face with a half-naked Luc Sanchis.

He was standing there watching her, and she went hot at the thought of him observing her so silently. He wore only a small white towel slung around very lean hips. A vast expanse of tautly muscled bronzed chest was in her eyeline, along with a very masculine dusting of dark hair.

Personally Jesse had never found the clean-chested look very enticing, and in response she could feel her nipples tightening into hard little buds. Broad shoulders drew her eyes upwards until she had to look into that ruggedly beautiful face. It was impassive. Not mocking, as she'd feared, after what had felt like her far too leisurely appraisal.

'I heard you taking a swim earlier.'

Jesse took a second to register his words. And then she nodded, slightly suspicious of this very sanguine Luc Sanchis. 'Yes…the pool is just through the French doors and down the garden. The other side of the bushes. There's a pool house stocked with robes and bathing suits.'

'Ah…' Luc folded his arms across that chest, making his muscles bunch. 'I did notice that in your kind kitting out of my *trousseau* there weren't any swimsuits. It doesn't matter, though. I prefer swimming naked. That is…if you think the owners wouldn't mind?'

A tide of heat swept up over Jesse's neck and throat at that image, but she managed to get out a garbled-sounding, 'No, I don't think so. The pool is cleaned regularly anyway. But, like I said, there are suits in the pool house.'

Luc had moved so that he was standing in the open doorway which led out to the fragrant night and the garden. Now Jesse had a full view of him from head to toe, and all she could see was that eye-wateringly small towel—which she feared might drop at any moment. Even though it was in her peripheral vision she noticed the very virile bulge of his manhood against the fabric, pushing it out. And she didn't doubt for a second that this was him *relaxed*.

He drawled, 'I think I'd still prefer to go naked.'

And with that he sauntered off into the gloom, with the moonlight casting long silvery shadows over everything.

Jesse blinked when she saw the lights come on around the pool and pool house. She could just make out the tall figure of Luc, and the flash of white as something was dropped or whipped away. And then there was a splash.

With a strangled sound Jesse whirled around and all but ran

from the kitchen up to her room. She closed the door firmly behind her and breathed deep, aghast at how fast her heart was beating. *How* and *why* was this man above all others affecting her like this? This was the least appropriate time for her to be feeling her hormones surge. She'd never needed her cool armour more than right now, to get through these next days and ensure the final demise of her father.

She'd blushed more since meeting Luc Sanchis than she'd ever blushed in her entire life. Even when she'd been intimate before she'd never felt this constant level of heat in her system, as if she had a kind of fever. She touched her forehead, but contrary to the rest of her, which felt as if it were burning up, it was cool. Betrayed by her own body. She hated it.

She pushed herself off the door and went to her securely locked case. Safe in the knowledge that she could still hear the faint splashes of Luc swimming, she opened the case and took out her phone, switching it on. Within minutes she'd dealt with some e-mails and had been informed that there were already headlines proclaiming that Luc Sanchis had backed out of his deal with JP O'Brien.

Jesse sent up silent thanks for the mole on O'Brien's staff who was giving her information. It was a disgruntled employee—a woman who had been sexually harassed by O'Brien but was too scared to jeopardise her job by coming out about it. Jesse had promised her that along with all of O'Brien's employees, apart from his close associates, she would be looked after when his business failed.

She switched off the device again and put it away securely. She took a deep breath. She couldn't hear the splashing any more. Luc Sanchis could be anywhere. But Jesse knew that as soon as he went near the perimeter fence, if he had half a mind to try to escape, all hell would break loose. She could rest easy and not care where he was so long as that didn't happen.

When she went into her bathroom, to shower before bed,

she tried not to notice the glitter in her eyes or her flushed cheeks, which told of something far more dangerous than satisfaction that her plan was working. And when she was naked under the teeming spray of her shower she tried desperately not to imagine Luc Sanchis as he might look now, after his swim, with water running in rivulets down those hard muscles…

Luc stood at the side of the pool, a large towel in one hand, letting the water drip from his naked body. The cool night air didn't bother him, even though his skin was in goosebumps, because he wasn't feeling cold. He was feeling quite *hot*.

A scowl marred his features momentarily, because he couldn't seem to bring his wayward body to heel. He looked down, almost bemused at the sight of his arousal which sprang rebelliously from his recalcitrant body.

He'd expected to go down to the kitchen and taunt Little Miss Uptight a bit. He hadn't expected that her blushes and obvious discomfiture would turn him on to the point where a cool dip in the pool had been entirely too necessary and annoyingly ineffective.

She'd looked all too appealing, standing there in bare feet and tight jeans, with a loose top half falling off one shoulder, exposing a very staid white bra strap. And her scent…that maddeningly inappropriate scent for one so uptight…had enflamed him even more. Making him think of an exotic harem scene, where she would be lying naked on a sumptuous divan.

In his fantasy she had long hair, spilling over her shoulders, tantalisingly touching small breasts which he imagined had nipples like hard berries, pink and ripe on his mouth and tongue…

Emitting a growl of frustration at finding himself thinking of *her* again, and not his predicament, Luc roughly rubbed the towel over his body and sent up silent thanks when his libido finally seemed to do as it was told. He slung the larger towel around his waist and turned off lights before striding back up the garden.

The villa's kitchen was still bathed in light, but he knew she was gone and, sure enough, when he glanced up he saw a light switch off in one of the rooms down from his.

He smiled grimly at the thought that Jesse Moriarty's crimes were mounting by the minute. The latest one being making Luc desire her.

The following morning Jesse was grouchy after a night of broken sleep. Even though she was well used to insomnia. She hadn't had a decent night's sleep for years, and it was in the small morning hours that she did her best work—even coming up with the anti-hacking software that had made her name. She was most relaxed when surrounded by quiet and darkness, such a far cry from her chaotic upbringing.

She cursed loudly as black smoke billowed out of the toaster and the kitchen's smoke alarm went off. Scrambling to try to eject the toast, she vaguely heard, *'What the hell?'* before she sensed a large presence by her side. And then she was being summarily lifted out of the way, so that Luc could flick out the charred toast far more dextrously than she'd been doing.

Even through the acrid smell of burning his own scent, clean and lemony, hit her nostrils and caused an immediate physical reaction. She lurched back further and took him in. He was now flicking a tea towel at the alarm, which was no bother to him considering his height. The T-shirt he was wearing pulled upwards, exposing a sliver of taut belly with that tantalising line of dark hair leading down under the jeans he was wearing. His bare feet, with their strong bones and hair-sprinkled toes, made Jesse's own feet curl into the tiled floor.

And then suddenly the alarm stopped, leaving the residue

of an echo in their ears as they adjusted to the silence again. A bird twittered innocuously outside.

Jesse gulped and looked up at Luc, who was quirking a brow and looking down at her with the offending toast held between thumb and forefinger.

'I didn't think it was actually possible to burn toast in a toaster. Obviously you're more proficient at computer programs and kidnapping.'

Jesse scowled at being reminded of the fact that in this area she failed miserably, and grabbed the toast out of his hand. She wasn't going to admit weakness in front of him now, and she slapped it down on a plate and took it over to the table, where a steaming cup of coffee awaited her.

'I don't have a sophisticated palate. I happen to like burnt toast.' She slathered spread on it defiantly, her stomach already protesting at the thought of eating it.

She took a bite and looked at Luc, who shrugged minutely as if already bored with her little performance. He said laconically, 'Forgive me if I don't join you—I prefer my food a little less *cooked*.'

She struggled to chew the burnt bread and watched as Luc busied himself pulling ingredients from the fridge. Eggs; salmon; milk… Then she continued to watch as he whistled tunelessly and prepared himself a delicious-looking breakfast of scrambled eggs and smoked salmon. All evidence was pointing to the fact that at least Luc wouldn't starve while on the island.

Seriously bemused to see this side of such a man, Jesse said faintly, 'There's some coffee in the pot.'

Luc grimaced slightly, and she watched as he took a sniff and then poured it down the sink before preparing a fresh one.

'No offence, but it would appear as if your coffee-making skills are in the same class as your toast-making skills.'

Inexplicably this made a dart of hurt lance Jesse. She'd

got so used to eating out of cartons or heating up ready-made meals for one that she hated to think of it as pointing to a lack in her life. A lack of something earthy and feminine. It made her think of her mother and how she'd used to love cooking up Irish stews and feeding them to her daughter, along with tales of growing up in the countryside in Ireland...

Before Jesse could get up and escape Luc came over to the table with his own breakfast and freshly brewed coffee, sitting down. Curiously she felt the urge to stay put, not to escape.

His breakfast mocked her. The scrambled eggs looked so fluffy she could imagine they tasted as light as air, and along with the strips of smoked salmon... Her mouth watered. And then the scent of fresh coffee hit her stomach and it rumbled.

Mortified, she knew her wish that Luc hadn't heard it hadn't been granted when he glanced up. He said, 'Help yourself to coffee, if you like...and there's eggs and salmon left over.'

Rigid with embarrassment, Jesse fought down the softening feeling inside and said caustically, 'I'm sure you don't really want to share food with your captor.'

Luc merely shrugged in a very Gallic way and said in between mouthfuls of food, 'I'm making the best of a bad situation. And I think if I can be pleasant then you certainly can. I'm the one here under duress, not you.'

Jesse felt ashamed, but bit back the words of apology on her lips. Unbelievably the man who wanted to save her father—one of the most corrupt men on the planet—was managing to make *her* feel in the wrong.

'You didn't attempt to escape last night?'

Luc finished chewing his last mouthful and looked at Jesse. He sat back and took a long sip of coffee, put his cup down.

He shook his head. 'No—as you well know. Because if I had the sensors would have set off the alarm and the sound of the sirens would have split our eardrums.' He elaborated.

'I have the same security system on several of my own properties. I know that it's so good it precludes the need for bodyguards. And I know how futile it would be to set it off.'

'Oh,' Jesse said now, still struck by how reluctant she seemed to be to leave. She was finding it curiously easy to be sitting across the table from the man she'd kidnapped the day before.

'Where did you learn to cook?'

Immediately a shuttered look came over Luc's face, his eyes going dark and mysterious. Jesse's gaze narrowed on him, her curiosity piqued properly now.

Luc regarded the woman across the table. She was in another loose top today, albeit a short-sleeved one. It showed off her slender pale arms and tiny wrists and hands. Immediately he was furnished with a graphic image of one of those hands wrapped around a certain part of his anatomy, and was rewarded with blood rushing to that strategic region in his pants. Curse her anyway.

Anger galvanised him into answering her, because this anger would help remind him of why it was so important to get out of here.

'I learnt to cook because my father died when I was twelve and my mother had a breakdown. I had to look after her and my younger sister.'

He saw Jesse's face blanch and her eyes grow wide. As if she cared.

Anger at her response spurred him on. 'My sister had—*has* special needs. She was deprived of oxygen at birth, and as a result has been mildly brain-damaged all her life. When my father died and my mother became ill she was only eight. She was terrified, so I had to try to keep things as constant as possible. Keeping her routine the same, including her meals, was part of that process. She's slightly autistic too, so any change in her routine was inordinately more threatening to her than to another person with the same needs…though she's much better now.'

Because, Luc reflected, he could now afford the best round-the-clock care and support.

Jesse's voice was husky, and it had an immediate effect on Luc's body. 'I'm sorry. It must have been a tough time.'

'The toughest,' he agreed grimly.

Suddenly he felt very exposed, sitting here and telling Jesse Moriarty, of all people, about the most cataclysmic time of his life, when all his anger and rage had coalesced into a lifelong ambition to see justice meted out.

'So how is it that you *can't* cook? I take it that burnt toast is just the tip of the iceberg?'

# CHAPTER FIVE

JESSE felt very vulnerable all of a sudden, and wondered if Luc had just furnished her with a fake story. But then she recalled the intensity on his face and in his eyes and she had to believe him—even though she didn't like the sympathy he'd evoked within her.

She looked down at the blackened remains on her plate and found herself saying, 'My mother died when I was nine. She was a brilliant cook, but she hadn't started to teach me yet... She kept saying she would but there never seemed to be time. She was so busy...' Jesse trailed off remembering her harried and stressed mother, whose face would be red and sweaty as she struggled to put together a meal for one of her father's dinner parties with the usual little or no notice.

One time when something had gone wrong he'd come downstairs, flushed in the face with drink, and slapped her mother so hard that she'd fallen over the kitchen table, bringing pots and plates to the floor, waking Jesse up.

Feeling seriously disorientated at having remembered that, Jesse forced it from her mind and said lightly, 'And then I just never learnt... I was terrible at home economics at school.'

'But brilliant at maths and computer sciences?'

Jesse glanced at Luc and shrugged minutely. 'They made more sense to me than sewing or baking.' She had lost herself in numbers and algorithms far more easily than the more *nurturing* classes.

'What about your father?'

Jesse forced her face to stay blank, not to respond. Tightly she said, 'My mother was a single parent; I never knew my father.'

She hadn't really. Not in the traditional sense. She'd always been the unwanted reminder downstairs. Hidden away. Until she'd had the temerity to come out and risk his wrath for the second time in her life. And that had had dire consequences.

Luc was moving and Jesse glanced up, a little disorientated to find that they'd been conversing so easily. He was heaping leftovers of egg and salmon onto his plate. He glanced at her and she felt breathless.

'Are you sure you don't want any?'

Jesse shook her head vigorously, realising that they'd gone way off track, sitting here talking relatively companionably. When Luc came back to sit down Jesse stood up and took her plate over to the sink to wash it. She felt prickly all over and, most betrayingly of all, as if she might cry.

Without saying anything to Luc she left the kitchen, walking as nonchalantly as she could, horribly aware that he might be looking at her. Only when she was around the corner and had ducked into the empty study that had so incensed him the day before did she breathe out shakily.

She walked to the window and looked over the stunning view of the garden at the side of the house. Crossing her arms over her chest, she told herself that she would have to be very careful not to trust this more civil side of Luc Sanchis. *Or* be moved by his stories of a difficult childhood. Her heart felt funny when she visualised him taking care of his vulnerable sister.

Jesse had to remember that he would be working tirelessly for a way to get off this island before he lost his chance to save

O'Brien. Undoubtedly he was up to something, and she'd be the biggest fool to forget that for a second.

That evening Luc was sitting in a chair on the terrace outside the kitchen. He'd just eaten a perfectly prepared steak with Béarnaise sauce and a salad, and was washing it down with a robust Merlot. He had to concede, much to his chagrin, that this enforced *doing nothing* wasn't entirely unwelcome. It had been a long time since he'd had no pressure on his time and energy. And it had been a long time since he'd indulged in cooking for himself. He'd forgotten how much he liked it.

He scowled faintly. Although he *hated* not being in control. When he'd watched Jesse saunter so nonchalantly from the kitchen that morning he'd wanted to send a cup flying after her to smash against the wall. To smash through that brittle shell that seemed to surround her all the time, making him want to delve underneath.

She made him feel all sorts of things, and he hated to acknowledge that anger at his kidnapping wasn't usually the uppermost emotion.

He heard a noise now and turned his head to see her in the kitchen. She'd been avoiding him all day. When he thought back to their conversation earlier he got the distinct impression that just as he'd spilled his guts far more than he'd intended so had she.

He hadn't missed the way she'd tightened all over at the mention of her father. Clearly that was a red button he should push again, seeking any means to unnerve her.

She'd obviously not seen him out on the terrace, and he sat back even more and observed her as she opened the fridge and took out the bowl of Béarnaise sauce he'd made. She lifted it to sniff and he found himself smiling at her wrinkled-nose expression. Curious as to what she would do with the raw materials in the fridge, he almost felt sorry for her when he saw her admit defeat and take out a yoghurt.

She had to be starving. Nothing had been moved from the fridge at lunchtime. Luc didn't like the feeling of protectiveness that came over him, and quashed it ruthlessly. A woman had inspired that in him before, and it had nearly cost him his burgeoning reputation and career. He certainly wouldn't give in to it here and now, with someone infinitely more dangerous.

Silently he stood up and went to stand with a shoulder propped against the open patio door, his eyes on the petite figure as she stood and ate the yoghurt.

'So, where have you been hiding all day? I missed you.'

Jesse went rigid as that deep, mocking voice washed over her and snuck in somewhere very private and vulnerable. She forced herself to be as cool as a cucumber before she turned around to face her nemesis. It was laughable, but right now she felt far more the victim than Luc Sanchis.

She could scent the tantalising aroma of something he'd cooked in the air. No doubt he must relish the thought of her starving.

He was standing with arms folded across his chest, one shoulder propped against the door. He jerked his head back to where he'd been eating. 'I made a steak. I didn't think to ask you if you wanted one. Call me old-fashioned, but I don't think the prisoner usually cares much about feeding the kidnapper.'

Jesse flushed and willed down the wave of hunger that almost knocked her sideways. She could well imagine that his steak had been as delicious as his breakfast. Churlishly she wondered if this was how he'd wear her down—by acute food envy. And why did the man have to be so proficient in the kitchen anyway? Why couldn't he conform and be some stereotypical male who was as blind in a kitchen as she was?

'Now, now—no need to look so fierce.' Luc straightened

up and went out, only to reappear seconds later with a glass of wine and a bottle. He tipped it towards Jesse. 'Wine?'

Jesse shook her head. On her empty stomach a glass of wine would be suicide. She backed away and said suspiciously, 'Why are you so cheery?'

Luc calmly poured some more wine into his own glass, and then came into the kitchen to put the bottle down on the counter-top. He took a sip.

'Like I said earlier, I'm making the best of a bad situation. As you pointed out, I can't hope to get off the island, and you're not going to let me near any means of outside communication, so what else can I do for the moment except feed myself and relax?'

Jesse recalled looking down from her bedroom that afternoon to see Luc stretched out in the family-sized hammock which was hung between two trees. He'd been bare-chested in those low-slung jeans, reading a book with an arm behind his head, showing off his pectoral muscles to great advantage.

She'd been transfixed for far longer than she cared to admit, with a slow upswelling of heat making beads of sweat pop out between her breasts before she'd realised what she was doing and moved away.

Abruptly, almost as if he'd touched her and she'd flinched, Jesse moved back. Angry. 'I'm not completely helpless, you know. I can make a sandwich or…something.'

She flung open the fridge door again and eyed a loaf of bread balefully. Resolutely she took it out, and then took out some cheese and mustard. Determined to show Luc that she wasn't to be pitied for being so culinarily challenged, she found a chopping board and set about cutting a slice of bread.

Perhaps it was his intent, mocking gaze on her, or the fact that she was left-handed, which always made her cut things awkwardly, having been brought up to use her right hand, but the knife slipped and sharp pain lanced her thumb, making her cry out.

Instantly she was aware of a blur of movement to her right, and then her hand was being cradled in a much bigger one and she was being led over to the sink. Already the awful numbing tide of sickness was coming over her at the sight of bright red blood. It got worse when Luc ran the water over the cut and she could see it flowing down the sink.

Sweat broke out on her brow as she fought back the wave of nausea. Blood had always sickened her. Ever since she'd seen her own blood running on the floor from the welts on her back and legs.

Seriously weak now, Jesse's legs were trembling violently. She felt rather than saw Luc cast her a swift glance.

'What's wrong with you? It's only a small nick.'

Jesse's tongue felt heavy in her head. 'The blood. I can't stand blood.'

Her legs gave way just as she heard Luc curse, and then she was being lifted against his hard chest and put down on a chair. His hand was on the back of her head, pushing it between her knees.

'Just breathe,' was his curt instruction.

She could feel him doing something to her thumb, wrapping something around it. Slowly the nausea was receding and her stomach was calming down.

She felt him move away from her and attempted to come back up, but he said roughly, 'Stay down until I say so or you'll get dizzy again.'

Jesse said nothing, just obeyed, too mortified to come up, too afraid to see what would be on Luc's face at her pathetic weakness. She couldn't cut a slice of bread without nearly cutting a finger off, and then she almost fainted. And, not only that, she was terrified of the response that had swept through her like a forest fire at being held so closely to his body as he'd all but carried her to the chair.

Eventually she saw his bare feet appear in her line of vision and heard something being put on the table behind her. She felt his hands on her arms and she was urged upwards. Her head swam for a moment, but then it cleared. Luc was looking down at her, his eyes searching her face.

Jesse could feel heat and colour rushing back. As if satisfied to see it, Luc propelled her chair around and she saw a plate with what looked like a steak sandwich on it and a glass of water.

Luc sat down on the chair nearest to her and motioned to her. 'Go on—eat. You need something in your belly.'

Jesse saw then that a plaster had been put on her thumb. It was throbbing a little, but there was no sight of blood, thank God.

She looked from the sandwich to Luc. 'I…I'm sorry. I don't know what…'

'Just eat.'

His voice was disarmingly gentle, doing funny things to her insides as she picked up the sandwich and took a bite. She nearly closed her eyes as the delicious taste of the meat hit her tastebuds. She'd never tasted anything so succulent and tender. She demolished it all in record time, and took a long sip of water before wiping her mouth with a napkin.

Luc was watching her with a slightly mesmerised look on his face. He shook his head. 'For someone so tiny you could put a mariner to shame, the way you eat.'

Jesse flushed and said, 'Just because I don't cook much for myself doesn't mean I don't have an appetite.'

Luc felt the slow lick of desire as he found himself wondering if Jesse's ravenous *appetite* ran to the more carnal kind. He watched her face and could see expressions flit across it like clouds scudding across a bay in high wind. Did she realise how transparent she was? Unless, of course, he mentioned a *verboten* subject like her father.

He was finding her more and more intriguing, and he was finding it difficult to focus on the fact that because of her his years of well-laid plans would all be for naught.

As if she could feel his intense regard, Jesse got up abruptly and took her things to the sink. Luc saw her hesitate for a second, as if afraid in case she saw blood again, but he'd been careful to wash it all away.

He didn't like the way his heart constricted slightly now. The line of her back looked incredibly delicate, and his eye travelled down over that T-shirt and the shorts she'd changed into during the afternoon. Her legs were smooth and pale. So slender he imagined wrapping a hand around one calf. And then he noticed something else: a long silvery line down one thigh that reached to the back of her knee, like a faded scar.

Just then Jesse turned, and he looked back up. Her face was a bland mask, and Luc held his tongue when what he wanted was to ask her about the scar. She'd retreated into her cool shell, and he had to curb the desire to stand up and walk over to her and kiss her.

He was disconcerted to find that as much as he wanted to do it to unsettle her, with a view to getting off this island, he also wanted to do it just for the sake of doing it.

Unwilling to explore this unwelcome desire, Luc stood up. His mood wasn't helped by the way Jesse's eyes widened fractionally, showing more of that dark grey intensity. Saying something vaguely coherent, Luc made for the door.

He stopped when he heard a tentative-sounding, *'Luc?'* He realised that it was the first time she'd said his first name out loud.

Feeling more and more threatened, he forced himself to turn around. He saw Jesse biting her lip before blurting out, 'Thank you...'

'It was nothing.' His voice was gruff. Disgusted, because he felt as if he was running away, he left and went to the sanctuary of his room.

Jesse sank back against the sink and looked at the empty doorway. Luc Sanchis had just been incredibly sweet to her. Since her mother died, she couldn't recall anyone being so nice to her—even making her a sandwich like that and sitting there till she ate it. In all of her foster homes invariably the parents had had children of their own, and more often than not had been stressed and busy. Jesse had often wondered why they'd bothered taking kids in when they couldn't seem to care for them properly...

Damn him, Jesse said to herself silently. She didn't want to *like* him. At all. She shook her head and made quick work of washing the plates—hers and Luc's—being careful to keep her thumb out of the water.

When she was finished she glanced at her watch and was surprised to see that it was already after ten p.m. A wave of tiredness washed over her, but Jesse felt the habitual frustration of an insomniac. If she went to bed now she would only wake in a couple of hours, and not get back to sleep until dawn.

Instead Jesse found herself searching through the DVDs in the den, and smiled when she found some computer games which she figured belonged to the Kouros children. Jesse recalled Alexandros telling her with a wry grin that their lives were dominated by their three boys. She gave thanks for their taste in games now, and settled down to play one of her old favourites.

When Luc had got back to his room he'd taken a shower and now lay on his bed in nothing but a towel. He tried to resist, but couldn't: the memory of how Jesse had felt leaning against him when she'd been overcome with weakness at the sight of the blood.

Her reaction had shocked him. She'd been so strong all along, despite the small signs of nerves and that damned air of vulnerability.

He could still feel the impression of her small firm breasts. When he'd helped her to sit up straight again he'd been able to see down the loose top of her shirt to the dewy skin of her cleavage. Her breasts had looked enticingly more full than he'd thought. And he'd felt like a teenager ogling his first woman.

He clenched his hands against the erection already growing and gritted his teeth. The first twenty-four-hour stretch of his incarceration had proved to him that this sexual awareness and frustration would only build. He was sure that it was heightened by the fact that Jesse was not his usual type, and further heightened by their enforced close proximity.

In normal circumstances he wouldn't find her so enthralling. But for now he did. And it would help him to achieve his aim. He would seduce her into revealing the secrets she hid in those flashing grey eyes. And then, when she was at her most vulnerable, he would have her and she wouldn't be able to deny him anything. Namely: his freedom.

When Luc woke around dawn he was still in the towel on the top of his bed. He was surprised as he had become accustomed to existing on three to four hours' sleep.

He had another quick shower and, feeling ridiculously refreshed, pulled on jeans from yesterday and a clean T-shirt, scowling at the open doors of the walk-in closet as he did so.

He'd never had a woman buy him clothes before. He'd bought plenty of clothes *and* jewellery for women, though, and had to wonder now why they liked it so much when it made *him* feel somehow soiled. He reflected with not a little irony that the women he lavished gifts on didn't give any impression of feeling soiled, and yet he could well imagine the distasteful look on Jesse Moriarty's face if he did such a thing...and he didn't like how that knowledge made him feel.

He closed the offending doors and padded downstairs in bare feet to the kitchen. He had to admit that under other circumstances he would properly enjoy this villa and the solitude. It was just unfortunate that he was confined within its perimeter fence and cut off from his life and livelihood.

Luc had almost walked past the den before he saw the small foot dangling off the sofa.

He stopped and went in, to see Jesse lying awkwardly on the couch, half-on and half-off, with earphones askew on her head. There was a console remote on the floor near her, and the TV was showing nothing but static.

Something within him moved at the sight of her, all tousled and sleep-flushed, her mouth in a delicious pout. Her T-shirt had ridden up to reveal a pale and very flat belly, her shorts sat low on slim hips.

He reached down and plucked the earphones off her ears. Jesse moved fractionally, whispering something under her breath that Luc couldn't quite catch. Before he'd really thought about what he was doing he'd slipped his arms under her, one under her back and the other under her legs, and lifted her against his chest.

Jesse was aware that she felt weightless against something hard, and that it wasn't an altogether unpleasant sensation. And then she became aware of more: a hard chest under her cheek, and someone's warm and minty-smelling breath on her forehead. Groggily she opened her eyes, to see that she was several feet off the ground and in Luc Sanchis's arms. She started to struggle, but it was ineffectual because she was still half asleep.

'Hold still. I'm just taking you up to your bed.'

His voice rumbled out from that chest, covered by only a flimsy T-shirt and Jesse was wide awake and as stiff as a board the time Luc walked her into her room and deposited her on her bed. To her dismay he didn't back away. He rested over her on his hands, the muscles in his arms far too close for comfort. As well as that huge body.

'I... Thank you. I must have fallen asleep.' Her voice sounded ridiculously husky to her ears.

*Please move away from me,* she begged silently, terrified of her body's response, which seemed to be worse because she hadn't yet woken up enough to censor it. That had to be why she wanted to reach out and curl her hands into the material of Luc's T-shirt and pull him closer so that she could—

As if hearing her chaotic thoughts, Luc *did* move closer then—and Jesse had nowhere to go as she was almost flat on the bed. Breathless, she asked, 'What are you doing?'

Half-musingly he said, 'Just checking something.'

And then he was dropping, coming closer, even though not a part of his body was actually touching hers yet. His face came so close to hers that it blurred in her eyesight and Jesse had to close her eyes. But that was worse because then she could smell him.

She was acutely aware of the fact that she was lying on her bed, with Luc Sanchis looming over her like a marauding pirate about to ravish her. And there was nothing she could do because she seemed to have been invaded by some fatal lethargy.

She felt the barest of touches, of his mouth to the corner of hers, before he moved down across the line of her jaw, and down again to where she knew her pulse must be beating hectically at her neck, betraying her like a beacon. She was drowning in his scent and the waves of heat from his body.

And then suddenly he was gone, and Jesse opened heavy

eyes to see Luc staring down at her with a smug look on his dark face, hands on lean hips. She only noticed then that his hair was still damp from a shower. Her insides tightened.

She sat up awkwardly, still feeling slightly uncoordinated, and then stood to face Luc, arms crossed over her chest and the betraying sting of her rock-hard nipples.

'What the hell do you think you're doing?'

Luc reached out and easily pulled Jesse's arms apart until she was standing there with her wrists manacled in his huge hands.

She strugged but couldn't break free. 'Let me *go*,' she demanded.

'What I was doing,' Luc said, in a supremely reasonable voice, 'was proving that you desire me.'

Jesse pulled against his hands to no avail. Anger at him for articulating her worst fear made her spit, 'Don't be ridiculous. You're the last man on this earth that I would desire. Maybe you were right. Maybe I *am* gay.' Jesse would have said anything right then to get him to back away.

'Really?' Luc glanced down to Jesse's chest, and to her abject horror and mortification she could feel her breasts swell against the confinement of her bra as if they literally ached for his touch.

'I don't think you're gay at all.' He dropped one of her hands, and she was so surprised for a second that she didn't stop him when he reached out and cupped one breast through the thin material of her T-shirt, and lazily rubbed a thumb back and forth over the covered peak.

Far too belatedly Jesse knocked his hand away and moved back well out of his reach. The ease with which he'd been able to hold her captive scared her, but it wasn't because she feared him being violent or forcing her. It was fear of the fact that she seemed to have no control around him.

Shakily she said, 'Get out of my room.'

Luc just smiled and held out his hands in a peace-making gesture. But he backed away, which had her breathing easier until he said, 'You only have yourself to blame for this, Jesse... It's your fault we're here on this island, alone together in this house.'

Jesse crossed her arms over her chest again and bit out, 'This villa is certainly big enough for both of us. Don't worry—I'll stay well out of your way.'

Luc's grin got bigger and momentarily blinded Jesse.

'I'm going to make some breakfast, if you'd care to join me?'

Jesse muttered something childish about preferring to eat worms, and it was only when Luc had finally walked out of her room and she'd hurried after him to close the door that she relaxed.

She looked at the lock on the door and wished with all her heart that she could turn the key—but she couldn't. Much like the sight of blood, she had a phobia about being locked into any room, thanks to her father...

Choking back the sudden rise of emotion, Jesse whirled away from the door and went to the bathroom, stripping off angrily before stepping under the shower. Realising that Luc had found her sleeping, the way she'd woken up in his arms and how that had felt, was seriously unnerving.

Luc Sanchis was playing with her because she'd been stupid enough to let him see that he affected her. This was his only weapon. So of course he was going to take advantage.

She would not let him fool her like this. He fancied her about as much as he fancied a block of wood. She'd seen his women on the internet—all buxom and glamorous and confident. Full of that innate feminine beauty that she'd never emulate.

Jesse turned her face up into the drumming spray to avoid thinking about how that made her feel.

* * *

Jesse managed successfully to avoid Luc for the rest of that day and evening. She wasn't sure how. She was just relieved that she had.

She'd gone down to the kitchen and picked at the leftovers of Luc's food, which had been helpfully left out on a covered plate on the counter. Jesse didn't want to acknowledge that he'd left them there for her but she had the uncomfortable feeling that he had.

All through the day the magnitude of what had happened that morning had grown bigger and bigger in her head, so that night was another sleepless one, spent tossing and turning. She got up to shower twice, in some kind of effort to relax. She even considered using the pool, but the thought of running into Luc made her stay in her room.

By the following morning she was worn out. She told herself she was being ridiculous. He was only playing with her head, trying to unnerve her, and she was letting him. All she had to do was draw on the cool shell of reserve that had served her so well for years. She told herself firmly to get a grip.

Dressing carefully in jeans and a shirt, all buttoned up, Jesse went down to the kitchen, girding herself to see Luc. And when she did all her recent good intentions melted into a heat haze. He was standing in the kitchen with his back to her, in nothing but a pair of board shorts which were slung low on his hips. The length of his olive-skinned bare back was a vision of muscled male perfection, drawing her helpless gaze all the way down to those lean hips. He was whistling tunelessly, with a tea towel thrown over his shoulder, and something smelt delicious.

# CHAPTER SIX

Luc sensed Jesse behind him, and something scarily exultant erupted in his chest as he fought not to turn around.

She'd avoided him the entire previous day and night—concrete evidence that he had her good and rattled. His mouth compressed. He'd been rattled enough himself after those moments in her bedroom. It had taken more restraint than he'd thought he possessed not to plunder her mouth there and then. And as for touching her breast…? He grimaced now, recalling the surge of arousal in his body at just that fleeting touch.

He saw a movement beside his feet and bent down. When he straightened up he turned around and affected his best expression of surprise.

When Luc turned around and saw her surprise was etched onto his face—except Jesse didn't believe it for a second. But then her attention was taken by the squirming tiny bundle of fur in his arms, held close to that bare chest. Curiosity defused her wariness instantly.

'What is that?'

Luc looked down, and then back to Jesse. 'It's a kitten. I found him wandering around the garden yesterday, so I gave him some milk and a wash and he's been here ever since.'

Jesse was helpless, walking towards them before she knew what she was doing. She and her mother had used to have a cat in her father's house, and once it had had a litter of kittens. When her father had found out he'd taken them all and told Jesse malevolently that he was going to put them in a sack and drown them in the river. Whether he had or not Jesse had never found out, but why wouldn't he? He'd done so much worse. She'd cried herself to sleep for a month after that incident.

Without even thinking about what she was doing she'd reached for and was stroking the tiny grey-striped tabby. It was horribly malnourished and scrawny, but his huge eyes broke Jesse's heart wide open.

'Where's the mother?' she asked huskily, too emotional to look up at Luc.

She saw Luc's wide shoulders shrug. 'She must have died—or else she would have come looking for this little one before now. Feral cats and dogs are all over Greece. The mother cat could have come onto the island on a boat, already pregnant... Here, hold him while I finish making breakfast.'

He handed the tiny bundle into Jesse's arms and she caught him to her, revelling in his warm weight, light as it was. The kitten snuggled into Jesse like the most trusting thing on the planet.

'I'm making an omelette. Would you like some?'

Jesse looked up at Luc then, and as much as she'd have liked to say no and insist on burning her own toast she was starving, and completely disarmed after seeing him cradling this tiny animal with such gentleness.

She shrugged. 'Okay...if you have enough.' She blushed when she thought of how she'd picked at his leftovers yesterday like some fugitive and turned away. She saw a box in the corner which Luc had obviously set up for the kitten, with paper at the bottom and some milk in a bowl.

He said from behind her, 'There's plenty.'

Jesse sat down on a chair and stroked the kitten, which was

purring happily now. Her chest felt tight. This was the last thing she'd expected when she'd steeled herself to see Luc.

He came over to the table after a couple of minutes and put down the fluffiest omelette Jesse had ever seen, with hot buttered toast on a plate beside it.

'Why don't you put Stripy in his box while we eat?'

Suddenly Jesse was awfully reluctant to let the kitten go, but she forced herself to get up and put him in the box, seeing him lap hungrily at the milk. When she came back and saw Luc sitting down with his own food she said, 'Stripy?'

Luc glanced at her. 'Well, he's grey and stripy...'

Jesse sat down and tried not to notice the expanse of Luc's bare chest. He was definitely doing this on purpose, and she was not going to react—even though she already felt hot and wanted to undo some buttons on her shirt.

'I think Tigger is a better name.'

When she didn't get a response she risked a glance at Luc, who was chewing his food.

He swallowed. 'Tigger?'

Jesse felt silly now. 'You know—after Tigger in *Winnie The Pooh*.'

'Wasn't he orange?'

Jesse shrugged, embarrassed, wishing she hadn't said anything. She took a mouthful of omelette and had to stop herself from moaning out loud. It melted on her tongue.

'Well, I don't see why he can't be Tigger too. Who says he has to be orange?' Jesse swallowed and looked at Luc. Something fluttered in her chest. 'It really doesn't matter. He's only a kitten...'

Luc watched as Jesse ducked her head again. Fascinating. The kitten had obviously moved her so much that it had melted the lines of tension he'd seen in her when he'd first turned around to greet her. He knew his bare chest was a bit much, but he'd been determined to make her as uncomfortable as possible.

And it would have worked if it hadn't been for the kitten. She'd softened instantly on seeing it. Transforming her. It was more than a little irritating that a small bit of fluff with four legs and a tail had managed to crack through Jesse's veneer quicker than Luc had.

With tension rising he finished his breakfast and sat back to watch Jesse finish hers. She cleaned her plate, and his chest tightened when he thought of how she'd taken some of the leftovers he'd left out yesterday.

He cursed himself. For God's sake, anyone would think *she* was the victim here! Time to stir her up a little.

He leant forward just as she was wiping her mouth, and he noticed the telltale way she moved back fractionally.

'Six more nights, Jesse.'

She leant back and pushed her plate away slightly, tense and suspicious. Avoiding his eye. 'What are you talking about?'

'I'm talking about the fact that there are six more nights to go in this villa, on this island, before you let me go.'

Jesse mentally counted in her head and then looked at Luc, determined to recover her equilibrium after the kitten had severely demolished it. She told herself stoutly that it had nothing to do with Luc.

'So what's your point?'

'My point, dear Jesse, is how are you going to get through the next few days and nights without admitting how much I affect you?'

Jesse snorted and stood up abruptly, reaching for Luc's plate and her own skittishly, making them crash together. She stalked over to the sink and busied herself clearing them and washing them. And then promptly dropped one back into the sudsy water when she felt a very large warm presence behind her and two very naked masculine arms snaked around her, caging her against the sink.

His heat and scent were all around her, and Jesse hated that her treacherous heart was thumping double-time. Her skin prickled with awareness and anticipation.

Luc's head came down near hers and he said softly, near her ear, 'Admit it, Jesse, you want me…'

Jesse turned abruptly within the cage of his arms and glared up at him, far too aware of that naked chest only centimetres away and that gorgeous mouth directly above hers. Lightning anger flashed up her spine at how weak he made her feel, at the power he had over her.

'Never, Luc Sanchis. I'll never admit such a thing because it's not true. You're deluding yourself. Do you think that you're some God-given gift to women? Well, you're not. You're very easily resistible, actually, and you can just stew in your own ego for the next six days for all I care.'

Jesse had wriggled out under his arm before he knew what she was doing and was almost out of his reach. But Luc caught her by the hand and pulled her back to him. He could feel the slender bones of her hand and wrist, and her inherent fragility only made him feel angrier.

'Damn it, Jesse, why is it so important that you get to have O'Brien?'

To Luc's utter shock and surprise he saw moisture glint in Jesse's eyes and she spat out, 'It just *is*, and I'll never tell you why. It's none of your business.'

Luc let her hand go, but brought both his hands to her arms, clamping them there and drawing her right in against his body—which was on fire now.

'You made it my business when you hacked into my life and brought me here with no means of escape, damn you.'

Jesse looked up into Luc's eyes and saw the burning flames

of anger in their depths. Her heart was beating so fast now that she felt dizzy. A desperate yearning was rising within her...to have him kiss her and make all those words disappear. It was so strong at that moment that it scared her to death.

Exerting all her strength, she pulled away from him. 'Just stay out of my way, Luc Sanchis...'

Jesse backed away out of the kitchen and Luc's voice was scathing. 'That's very mature, Jesse. Are you going to hide in your room for another twenty-four hours?'

Jesse turned and fled, her emotions in turmoil. She *was* seriously tempted to go up to her room, but his caustic words made her go out through the front door instead. Impulsively she took the key to the Jeep from its secret spot and started it up with a shaking hand. She headed down the drive and through the gates, clicking the button to make sure they were shut again.

And her dominant feeling as she drove away from the villa, leaving Luc behind, locked in, was one of searing guilt.

She finally got to the edge of the airstrip and stopped, pulling over at a skewed angle. She all but fell out of the Jeep and stood in the bright morning sunlight, breathing deeply. Her heart was still hammering. It was as if Luc had reached inside her and effortlessly tied her insides into a knot, while at the same time making her melt as if she were made of nothing more than putty.

The truth was, right now she didn't know if she could last another week with Luc tormenting her. He had no idea how close he was to the truth of how much she wanted him to touch her...it was getting worse with every moment spent in his company. Once again *she* was feeling more like the prisoner.

*Why* couldn't she be immune to him? *Why* was he proving to be the one man on the planet who made her feel anything but cold inside? It was so demoralising to be one of the legion of women who fell at his feet in sighing ecstasy. And why had he had to tell her about his vulnerable younger sister with special needs, and how his mother had become ill after his father's death?

She thought churlishly that he would make a good model for one of those posters of men holding tiny vulnerable things like babies…or *kittens*.

Immediately Jesse felt trembly again. And emotional. She'd been blocking out emotions for so long now she almost didn't recognise the tight feeling which got tighter and tighter until she felt moisture running down her face and recognised tears.

She hadn't cried in years. Not since she'd retreated to a numb place where nothing could hurt her after her mother died. The same numb place her ex-lover had failed so spectacularly to melt. And yet within days of spending time with Luc Sanchis she was blubbing uncontrollably and melting all over.

Jesse fiercely wiped the tears from her cheeks and blew her nose. She had to get it together. This was exactly what he was trying to do—make her crumble so that she'd give in and send for the plane to take him back. She was so close now to her goal. She couldn't fall at the final hurdle.

Resolutely, after a few shuddering breaths, Jesse got back into the Jeep, turned it around and went back to the villa.

Luc had finished a punishing round of lengths in the pool and was walking back up through the garden, a towel slung casually around his waist. He tensed when he saw Jesse sitting cross-legged in the distance, just outside the kitchen doors, playing with the kitten. For a second he was almost tempted to laugh: his gaoler could hardly present a more benign image. And then he scowled. Because she was all too effective as a gaoler.

He came closer and saw the unmistakable lines of tension come into her body. He cursed inwardly. He didn't know why it was, but he'd felt like a heel when she'd all but run from the kitchen earlier. She'd seemed genuinely upset. But he knew he had to knock these weak impulses on the head. It was all an act, designed to keep him off balance. The woman had kidnapped him to further her own nefarious ends. She was about as vulnerable as a poisonous cobra!

When he reached her she said, without glancing up, 'Is our milk okay for Tigger?'

He reacted inexplicably to *our*. Her voice had sounded husky, reminding him of how his sister's voice sounded after she'd been crying. *Had she been crying?* Luc tensed at the hollow feeling in his belly.

'It isn't ideal, but it's all we have… He looks too small to eat anything solid yet.'

The kitten at that moment scrambled out of Jesse's hands and bounded over to Luc's bare foot. He reached down and scooped it up in one hand, aware of Jesse valiantly ignoring him and fixing something in the box nearby.

Eventually, giving up on Jesse actually looking up at him, and aware that her proximity even in that shirt and jeans was having an effect on him, he handed the kitten back to her, holding out his hand.

She reached up, slightly akwardly because she wouldn't meet his eyes, and took the kitten. An electric shock zinged between them when their fingers touched and Luc's jaw tensed. He quashed any weakness at hearing her husky voice.

*Ignore that at your peril,* he told her silently in his head, and finally went back into the villa, thoroughly irritated by everything about Jesse Moriarty.

Jesse breathed a deep sigh of relief. She'd emerged from that encounter relatively unscathed, thanks to the fact that she just hadn't looked at Luc. But she couldn't very well behave like that for the rest of the week. She had to keep drumming it into her skull that he was out to get her and to torture her. She had to resist him at all costs.

Feeling sticky and hot in her jeans and shirt, Jesse decided to have a swim too. At least the pool would be safe now that he'd finished. She carefully put Tigger back in his box and watched him curl up into a tiny ball of fluff, envying him his ease at being able to shut out the world and depend on the kindness of strangers.

Jesse went upstairs to get her swimsuit, and was passing Luc's bedroom door when she heard a sound. Without thinking, she glanced in. She could see right through the open door to his bathroom, where his tall and tautly muscled form was stepping out of the shower. *Completely naked.*

Jesse stopped in her tracks. She couldn't seem to take her eyes off his body. She'd never seen anything so perfect. Water droplets clung to taut muscles. Not an ounce of fat marred the lean lines. He had stopped too, and was looking right back at Jesse, totally unselfconscious in his nudity.

After a long moment, during which Jesse forgot how to breathe, Luc casually reached for a towel and held it over his penis, doing little to erase the image of the dark thatch of hair which cradled his impressive masculinity. Jesse knew it would be burnt onto her mind like a tattoo for ever.

When she noticed her lungs screaming she took in a deep breath and then, issuing a strangled sound, she reached for Luc's door to close it.

Just before she did, she heard him say mockingly, 'You're the one who stopped to look, Jesse.'

She slammed the door on his incendiary image and was out and down by the pool before she realised she'd never picked up her swimsuit. Beyond angry with Luc, and herself, and everything at that moment, Jesse rebelliously stripped off completely and dived into the pool.

She realised her folly only when her limbs were shaking

with exhaustion and she stopped to come up for air—and saw Luc hunkered down by the side of the pool. He looked very fresh, with his damp hair slicked back, and was dressed in chinos and a shirt. He had a towelling robe in one hand.

'If I'd known you were going to skinny-dip I would have waited to join you.'

The recent image of him fully naked and so potently masculine made Jesse's anger surge all over again. She crossed one hand over her breasts and held out the other, making sure to stay under water, where her body would be distorted enough not to give him a clear view. At least it was dusky now, which would also hide a multitude.

Luc straightened up then, to go and stand by the steps which led out of the shallow end of the pool. He held out the robe just over the water. To get to it Jesse would have to walk up a few steps stark naked. She fumed and cursed silently. This was all her own fault. If she hadn't acted like a teenager after seeing him naked she'd be perfectly decent in a one-piece swimsuit.

'It's only fair, Jesse,' he cajoled softly. 'After all, you saw me naked.'

She spluttered indignantly. 'Only because you left your doors open so I couldn't fail to notice you.'

He shook his head and chuckled softly—and that did all sorts of things to Jesse's equilibrium. 'Do you really think I went to all that trouble just in case you walked past at that exact moment?'

Jesse flushed even as goosebumps popped up on her exposed skin. No, she could very well imagine him nonchalantly shedding his towel and stepping into the steaming shower, not caring who saw him.

'Come on,' he said more briskly. 'You're going to freeze.'

Jesse's teeth were already starting to chatter; it was cool in the evenings here, with hot summer still a few months away. Gritting her jaw, and feeling more exposed than she'd ever been in her life, Jesse stepped forward and then up the steps out of the pool. She grabbed the robe out of Luc's hands.

She put it on awkwardly, and as every nano-second passed with torturous slowness was aware of his eyes on her bare skin. She could have wept when one arm of the robe proved to be stubbornly impossible to find, and stilled when Luc came forward and found it, helping to thread her arm through.

He came in front of her then and pulled the lapels of the robe together, covering her. Jesse belted it firmly, feeling the awful onset of weak tears *again*. She couldn't curse Luc any more than she already had. She felt a finger tipping up her chin and gritted her jaw against his hand, her eyes flashing brilliantly in the gloaming light.

Luc was speechless for a long moment. Seeing Jesse emerge from the pool just now…he'd never witnessed such delicately feminine perfection. She was small-boned and tiny-waisted. But her hips flared out from her waist in such a way as to make him ache to put his hands there and mould their shape to his. The small tangle of strawberry-blonde curls covering her sex had made his mouth go dry.

Her breasts were fuller than he'd thought, and firm, with small nipples, tight and hard from the water and pink against her pale skin.

She was looking up at him now, eyes huge in her heart-shaped face, hair slicked back. No make-up. A wealth of emotion brimmed in those grey pools, and Luc was falling into a place he'd never been before.

The words came out of his mouth before he realised he'd even registered them. 'You're beautiful.'

He knew then that he'd said them many times before to other women but never really meant them as he did now.

For a second Jesse couldn't respond. She was in thrall. To this moment and this man, and the way he'd pulled her robe closed with a kind of proprietorial gentleness, and then the way he'd said *You're beautiful.*

A bird called loudly nearby and the spell was abruptly broken. Humiliation washed over Jesse. He was doing it again—mocking her. The man deserved an Oscar for his performace.

She pulled away and stepped back. 'Stay out of my face, Sanchis.'

And with that she turned and walked back up to the villa, stopping herself from breaking into a run.

Luc watched her small form, the flash of bare pale legs in the gloom. She stopped by Tigger's box inside the kitchen door and his own hands clenched into fists at his sides when he imagined those small hands running over the kitten. He wanted those hands running over *him*. All over his body and particularly where he ached most.

Luc set off back to the villa once he knew Jesse would be in her room. He didn't doubt he wouldn't see her again this evening. She was as skittish as a foal. He wondered what had made her like that. She had to be at least twenty-five, if not older…

Forget about torturing *her*, he thought grimly. The only person he seemed to be torturing was himself. She'd been lucky she'd caught him coming *out* of his shower earlier, or else she'd have seen the full extent of how easily she turned him on…

Through the tangled haze of frustration in Luc's brain he had to face the uncomfortable realisation that no other woman had made him feel this hot. Not even Maria, and she had consumed him day and night for weeks.

Even though he could acknowledge now that his youth and inexperience had had a lot to do with how easily she'd seduced him, it didn't take away the burn of humiliation. He'd been obsessed with her. He'd believed that perhaps everything wasn't always meant to be tragic and sad. And Eva, his sister, had been enraptured with her too, captivated by her beauty and the long, luxurious fall of her glossy chestnut hair.

Luc felt sick inside when he recalled that final ugly day, when the extent of how naive he'd been and how ugly Maria really was had spilled out. She'd shuddered visibly and said, *'And as for your sister—how can you tolerate her in your family? She's not even all there—and the way she wants to touch me all the time and play with my hair...it disgusts me.'*

Luc felt guilty to this day that he'd allowed her near his beloved sister. He thought of Eva and his mother then, and suddenly resented Jesse bitterly for putting him in a position where he might not be contactable in case they needed him.

Anger at that, and anger at the way she was making him feel in general, fuelled him. He bounded up the stairs to Jesse's room to knock brusquely on the door.

He heard faint movements inside, and then the door opened to reveal her fresh from the shower, with another robe on and a towel around her head. That heady scent that was uniquely hers reached out and wound around him like a siren's call, bringing with it all sorts of images of tangled sweaty bodies.

He fought against it and gritted out, 'I need to call my messaging service to check if everything is okay and in case my mother or sister have been trying to reach me.'

Jesse opened her mouth but before she could say anything Luc had planted a hand high on the doorjamb. 'You'd better let me do this, Jesse,' he said ominously. 'Or else this becomes about a lot more than just O'Brien. I have many more business interests other than him, but if my mother or sister need me and I don't know about it then you will regret the day you were born.'

Jesse looked up into dark, hard eyes and felt ice slither down her spine for the first time since she'd brought Luc to the island. When it came to his mother and sister clearly he really meant it. For a treacherous moment Jesse wondered what it would be like to have someone that protective of *her*.

Almost as much to deny that rogue feeling as to give in to fear, Jesse muttered, 'Fine. I don't see how that's not fair.' Especially as she'd been checking on her own business concerns whenever she had a chance. She looked up at him. 'But we do it my way, and I'll supervise every moment. If I think you're sending someone a message then I'll terminate the connection immediately.'

'Fine.' He was curt.

'I'll get changed and come down in a minute.'

She closed the door in his face and quickly threw off the towels, dressing in loose cargo pants and a white shirt. She didn't bother with a bra, and rubbed her hair briskly and went back outside. She wasn't wholly surprised to see Luc waiting for her, arms crossed and leaning back against the opposite wall, eyes heavy-lidded and dangerous.

She walked ahead of him down the stairs and to the door of the study, very aware of her lack of a bra now and regretting her haste.

She turned around and looked up at Luc. 'Wait here.'

She went in and closed the door, jiggling the lock to make it sound as if she'd locked it, then hurried to the safe where she took out the landline phone. She plugged it in and re-locked the safe, and then went back and did the same thing again to the lock. She hated these weaknesses: a phobia of blood and locked rooms.

She opened the door and admitted Luc.

His gaze immediately narrowed on the phone, and he quirked a brow at her. 'What's to stop me from overpowering you and making the relevant calls to get me rescued?'

'Nothing,' Jesse admitted. 'But you wouldn't get very far, because there's a twelve-digit security code you need to put in before any external calls can be made.'

His eyes flashed. 'And I guess you're not going to divulge it.' It wasn't a question.

Jesse said nothing, just stuck her chin a little higher, determined not to let him intimidate her.

'Go on, then,' he bit out. 'Put it in.'

Jesse went to the phone and covered her hand, putting in the code. A photographic memory was one of the quirky traits that had helped her get a scholarship to Cambridge.

She held out the phone to Luc when she heard the outside dial tone. He took it and glared at her, before punching in the number for his messaging service. Jesse had moved to where the phone was connected to the wall, so she could easily pull the connection out if required.

She saw him register the messages and punch in the relevant numbers to retrieve them. He pulled a notepad and pen to him and wrote some things down. Then he terminated the call himself and looked at Jesse. 'Not surprisingly there are lots of irate calls from O'Brien's people, wondering what the hell is going on,' he said caustically.

Jesse couldn't even really feel satisfied. She felt numb inside when she thought of that man.

She was about to pull the connection from the wall when Luc said, 'Wait. I want to call my sister and give her another number to call in case there's an emergency.'

Jesse battled with her conscience. She couldn't absolutely trust that Luc's story about his background was true, but what if it was? What if his sister needed him?

Reluctantly she came over and wrote a number down on a piece of paper. 'Give her that number. If she calls I'll let you know.'

She put in the twelve-digit number again and Luc made his call. Jesse resumed her spot by the wall connection and waited with bated breath for Luc to blurt something out to his secretary or someone else. But instead he turned away from her and she heard him leave a message.

'Eva, *cariño*, it's me. I hope you and Mama and George are having a wonderful trip. In case something comes up and you can't get through to me straight away on my regular number I have another one...'

He listed off the numbers and then said softly into the phone, 'I'll see you soon, *querida*, take care of Mama. *Adiós.*'

Jesse saw his hand come down to terminate the connection, and as soon as he did so she took the cord out of the wall and came back, wrapping it around her hand.

Luc turned around and put his hands down on the desk, leaning forward. His face was suddenly close to Jesse's and the breath stalled in her throat. He brought a hand up and traced her jaw with a finger, making her skin tingle all over.

'You will pay for this, Jesse Moriarty... I will find out all your secrets and you will pay...'

Jesse jerked her head back. 'I don't have any secrets, Sanchis.'

He stood up and shook his head, and said mock sternly, 'It's not *Sanchis* any more, Jesse. It's Luc; we've gone way too far to go back now.'

With that he turned and left the room. Jesse hugged the phone to her chest for a long moment. She felt ridiculously emotional because the truth was that she had no one to call. No one who really cared where she was, or with whom. Luc's words floated back to her. *We've gone way too far to go back now.*

As she put the phone back into the safe and locked it again, Jesse pushed down the prickling sense of foreboding.

When she went into the kitchen a little later it was empty, but pans were in the sink—evidence of Luc's dinner. She tried not to feel hurt that he hadn't offered her anything, and then realised how ridiculous that was when he was her prisoner and owed her nothing. But somehow in the past couple of days she'd almost got used to Luc thinking of her needs too.

She found some cheese and bread in the fridge and managed to make a passable sandwich without maiming herself this time, sitting down to eat it at the table, with Tigger running back and forth by her feet. Jesse couldn't help but smile at the antics of the tiny kitten. Despite its very obvious malnourishment it was so...*ebullient*, as if it hadn't realised the precariousness of its own survival.

When she was finished she washed up, including Luc's pans, and filled Tigger's bowl with more milk. She replaced the papers with fresh ones and put him back in the box, where he curled up.

Jesse put her hands on her hips and sighed, looking down at him. And then, feeling curiously restless and wondering where Luc was, she went back through the house. There was no sign of Luc, but Jesse knew he wouldn't be far because it was dark outside and the alarm was on.

She sat down on the couch and saw the fallen console from the other night. Within a few minutes she'd set up the game and was happily ensconced in the fantasy world of *Final Retribution: to the Death*.

Luc stood watching Jesse from the doorway. She was oblivious to anything but the game she was engrossed in, her fingers flying with almost inhuman speed over the controls on the console. There was a tiny frown between her eyes and, as much as Luc wanted to deny it, it was adorable. With her legs crossed and in bare feet, she looked like a tousle-haired sexy elf.

The anger that had been fuelling him earlier had dissipated a little. It was as if he'd only then allowed the enormity of how powerless he was to hit him—when he'd thought about his mother and sister and realised that he wouldn't know if they needed him. The most enraging thing about that was that it hadn't been his uppermost concern from the start. Because this woman had taken up every space in his head—and his libido.

His mouth settled to a grim line now as he took her in. There was only one way he could think of to assert some dominance in this situation and it had been far too long coming… It was time to give Jesse Moriarty a little taste of feeling out of control for a change.

# CHAPTER SEVEN

JESSE'S skin prickled and her concentration faltered for a second when she sensed Luc's presence in the room. She glanced up and saw him prowling towards the sofa. Before he got there he reached down and picked something up. It was the other game console.

He sat down beside her, far too close for comfort, and smiled at her. His weight meant that she fell towards him and Jesse quickly scrambled back, out of the danger zone, putting some space between them.

She tried not to be blinded by his smile and asked a little too breathily, 'Did you want something?'

He looked at her for a long intense moment that had a very predictable effect on her heart-rate, and then sat back and said lazily, 'This is a game for two, isn't it?'

Jesse felt stiff and prim, and severely threatened. 'Yes, but I'm playing both parts and I'm on one of the highest levels...'

'So what...? Are you saying I can't join in? You did say you wanted me to be as comfortable as possible here.'

Jesse didn't trust this wide-eyed innocence for a second. She wanted to snap back, *That doesn't mean smiling at me and walking around half-naked at any given opportunity and making me want you.*

Shock as those last few words registered in her brain made

Jesse blurt out, 'Fine. We'll start a new game, I'm Princess Olga…you can be King Ordak.'

Luc tutted. 'Just because I'm the man I have to be King Ordak?'

Jesse rolled her eyes. 'Fine, *you* be the Princess and I'll be Ordak.'

'Does this mean I get to take off your head?'

The unmistakable light of challenge lit Jesse's eyes. 'You can try.'

'Brave words, King Ordak, brave words…'

Jesse had lost track of time about three games later. She'd expected to walk all over Luc, but he'd caught on to the rules faster than anyone she'd ever seen and had just subjected her to a particularly brutal death by skewering her with a wooden pole.

'You don't have to look so pleased with yourself,' she grumbled—and then was taken aback to discover that she was not only having something that approximated *fun* but also once again she was feeling comfortable with Luc.

Before she could really register that, he said easily, 'You don't seem to mind the blood in these games.'

Jesse tensed at being reminded of her weakness and how gentle he'd been with her. 'No,' she said carefully. 'I know it's not real.'

She made sure not to look at him, very afraid he'd see something on her face or in her eyes. This whole situation was careening wildly out of control.

'One more game.' He sounded determined.

'Just so you can try to beat my score?' Jesse asked lightly, glad Luc wasn't pursuing the subject of her phobia of blood.

Luc sat back and Jesse was aware of his arm stretched out on the couch behind her. When had they moved closer together?

He drawled, 'One more game and this time let's up the ante a little—see how good you really are.'

Jesse cursed herself for not being able to get up and walk away from the danger she scented in the air, but she couldn't resist a challenge. It was one of the reasons she'd done so well—because people had consistently told her that with her background she'd amount to nothing.

She glanced at him warily and hated to admit her attention was piqued. It made her bite out, 'What do you mean?'

Luc came forward and Jesse's gaze followed him suspiciously. The intent in his eyes made her hot in the face.

'If I win, you let me do whatever I want…' His mouth twisted. 'I realise that doesn't include letting me off the island or making a call to that end.'

Jesse racked her brains. *Whatever he wanted*… That could be anything. But as long as it didn't involve freeing him what was the harm?

Some of her equilibrium returning, Jesse said, 'But you won't win. So what do I get when I win?'

Dryly Luc observed, 'I think you've got quite enough, don't you?'

Jesse scowled and then brightened. 'I know. You can cook for me for the rest of the week.'

Now Luc scowled. 'I'm practically cooking for you anyway, so that's hardly fair… But, fine, if that's what you want.'

Jesse stuck out her hand and then immediately regretted it when it was enveloped in his much larger one. Luc seemed to hold her hand for ever, and she finally pulled free and turned back to the game. She had a prickle of foreboding as to what Luc might exact from her if she won and she couldn't allow him any leeway to torture her further.

The game started and Jesse scored a few easy victories, which made her feel complacent and which inevitably led to mistakes. Before she knew it Luc had caught up with her score and then they were neck and neck. All Luc had to do was to kill her in one of three ways and he would win.

Just as Jesse realised that, Luc made a master move she didn't see coming, and she watched in disbelief as her body was ripped in half, with cartoon-style blood gushing everywhere. She was speechless. No one *ever* beat her at computer games. In the geek world she was legendary, and had an unbroken record.

Until now.

She felt the console being taken out of her hand and Luc cleared his throat. 'So, where were we?'

Jesse looked at him blankly, aware of his very smug expression. She couldn't help admitting, 'I can't believe you just did that.'

'You're not the only one who has obviously racked up many misspent hours playing computer games.'

Jesse rounded on him properly. 'You should have told me! That's unfair, because I wasn't playing to full capacity! If you're as good as that, then—'

'Ah-ah.'

Luc put a finger to Jesse's open mouth. She closed it abruptly, but not before she'd got a tantalising taste of warm skin. He took his finger away, much to Jesse's relief—because she'd had an absurd urge to suck it.

'Don't be a sore loser, Jesse, it's not attractive. I think it's clear who *has* won the game and according to the terms we agreed, you have to let me do whatever I want.'

Her heart was thumping crazily. The game was forgotten. Jesse looked at Luc with a kind of mounting mixture of anticipation and horror. Her voice was scratchy. 'What…what is it that you want?'

Luc's gaze travelled over Jesse's face, lingering on her mouth, which tingled in reaction, dipping down to her chest, where she imagined he could see right through to the bare skin of her breasts, and then back up. He was like a lazy panther, with all the time in the world to catch his prey.

'What I want to do, Jesse, is kiss you.'

Jesse instantly recoiled backwards. 'Don't be ridiculous. You don't want to kiss me.'

Luc closed the distance between them, his gaze fixated on her mouth—which Jesse had always thought of as exceedingly *un*sexy, but which now felt disturbingly provocative.

'Oh, yes, Jesse, I do.'

'No.' Jesse was shaking her head and scrambling back further along the couch, horror and awful anticipation solidifying in her belly. 'You don't.'

With seemingly effortless ease Luc merely came closer again, until Jesse was all but crouching in the corner of the spacious comfy couch, knees drawn up to her chest, eyes huge, heart thumping out of control. A fine sweat was breaking out all over her body and all she could see was Luc Sanchis, broad and dark and infinitely more dangerous to her than anything she'd ever known before in her life. Including her father.

'Please don't…'

Luc ignored the way his chest tightened at that plea and those huge eyes as he came close enough to form a cage around Jesse, with his arms either side of her. She was pale, with two spots of pink in each cheek, her chest rising and falling rapidly. He couldn't stop now, because this was exactly how he wanted her: trembling and vulnerable.

He needed to establish some control, and he wanted to stamp some dominance onto this whole scenario. But curiously, as he stared into those stormy grey eyes, all those iron-clad intentions seemed to fade away…and what he wanted was much less coherent.

Luc snaked a hand around the back of Jesse's head, fingers massaging her neck, tangling in luxuriously soft, silky hair. He cupped her skull, feeling how fragile it was and desire surged in his body. He could feel the tremors going through her legs against his chest, and suddenly overriding everything became a need to soothe. He was a little blindsided by how much he wanted to put her at ease—and it wasn't just about the endgame. Something more was happening. It was as if he sensed a deep vulnerability within her.

He heard himself say, 'It's okay, Jesse. I'm not going to hurt you... I wouldn't do that.'

Inexorably he urged her mouth closer to his and closed the distance between them...

Jesse struggled to keep her eyes open, but the dark brown pools of Luc's eyes were pulling her down. She knew on some rational level that she should kick her legs out, push him away, because she sensed that he wouldn't force her...but she didn't. She was her own worst enemy.

As soon as she'd had the vaguest suspicion that this was what he wanted excitement had bubbled through her veins, along with that fear and trepidation. On some level she suspected she'd known all along what he might want, but weakly she'd not acknowledged it. Had she even *let* him win? The thought was too huge to acknowledge.

What she did know was that since she'd seen him at that event a year ago, and he'd looked down into her eyes with that piercing regard, she'd imagined a moment like this. And she'd been transparent enough at the time to let him see it. And now it was going to happen, and she couldn't, didn't, want to stop it.

Luc's mouth touched hers and it was like getting a thousand tiny electric shocks at once. He drew back slightly, as if he'd felt it too. Jesse's eyes flew open and clashed with molten brown. They were almost accusatory, as if she'd done something wrong, but before she could articulate anything Luc was slanting his mouth over hers again and kissing her forcibly, his hand holding her head captive.

Jesse knew she was fighting a losing battle to try to pretend she was unaffected—not when she yearned for Luc's mouth to be harder on hers. With a groan of angry supplication Jesse opened her mouth a fraction and Luc took advantage of her capitulation. Within what felt like seconds their mouths were both open, tongues touching and tasting, dancing forward and retreating back.

Luc's hand gently angled Jesse's head to give him deeper penetration and her insides caught fire; her toes curled against the material of the couch. She could feel the solid steel wall of Luc's chest against her legs and wanted to open them, to bring him closer.

They kissed for long, timeless moments, one second passionately intense, the next languid and almost lazy, with Luc nipping at the corner of Jesse's mouth. She was vaguely aware of Luc manoeuvring her, but was too intent on tasting him, revelling in his musky scent and that wicked tongue.

When Luc did pull back for a moment Jesse was mortified to find that she'd followed him, as if loath to let him go. And then she realised that she was lying back against Luc's arm, and that he'd shifted them so that her legs were now draped over his lap and his free hand was on her belly.

She felt completely dazed and disorientated. Boneless. As if some seismic shift had happened within her. She couldn't even drum up anger right now. *This*—she craved this like a starving person craved food. This physicality was a need she'd denied for too long, her whole life. For someone who lived so much in her head, suddenly it was all about her body and what *it* needed. All she could do was lift a hand and touch Luc's hard jaw, tracing its contours with her fingers, marvelling at how pale her skin was next to his.

Luc's voice sounded thick and slightly slurred. 'I want to see you, Jesse...'

His hand moved up to the buttons on her shirt. Jesse's belly tightened with delicious anticipation. She bit her lip and it was swollen. All she knew right then was that she didn't want this moment to end. She'd been transported too far into a new seductive world to turn back.

She felt a fleeting moment of panic as sanity threatened to break through the fog in her brain and tensed minutely. But when she searched Luc's eyes, as if she would find something to help pull her out of this quicksand, she saw nothing but her own desire mirrored there. Shyly she nodded her head with one little jerk, and the flash of heat in Luc's eyes gave her a heady sense of confidence and—worse—*reassurance*.

*Trust him,* her body was crying out, seeking fulfilment. And Jesse realised that she wanted to more than anything.

This was so far removed from her previous experience with a man that she had no frame of reference for anything except knowing that she wanted to go forward. Luc's long fingers moved to the top button of her shirt and Jesse shivered when he opened it. She felt the backs of his fingers against her skin, then she thought of something and stopped his hand with hers.

Their eyes met and she said, 'I don't… I'm not wearing a bra.'

Luc smiled and it was pure sin. 'I noticed…'

Jesse's insides melted along with any doubts. She dropped her hand and for the first time in her life felt *sensual*. Luc's eyes went back to her shirt and his fingers made fast work of undoing her buttons until her shirt gaped open slightly. Reverently, Luc pushed the material aside to reveal one breast, and Jesse sucked in a breath, unwittingly making her breast swell.

Two slashes of colour lined Luc's cheeks and Jesse was desperately biting inside her mouth. She wanted him to touch her so badly. And then he did, and she almost arched off the couch.

All Luc could see was a red haze of lust. He heard nothing

but a dull pounding in his ears and was vaguely aware that it was his heart. Jesse's breast fitted into his hand as if made for it. Her hard nipple scraped his palm and he had to bite back a groan. He squeezed the firm flesh, making her nipple even harder, and then he couldn't wait any longer. He bent his head and surrounded that tight pointed peak in hot moisture, rolling and flicking his tongue around it, biting gently.

He could feel Jesse moving with a response she couldn't hide, and that sent Luc's levels of arousal into orbit. The fact that this was surpassing anything he'd experienced with a woman before was something he was in no position or state of mind to think about or acknowledge.

Jesse had never known this drugging, all-encompassing feeling. It was exquisite and torturous all at the same time. She wanted Luc both to stop and never to stop. When he pushed her shirt apart completely and administered the same attention to her other breast she was no longer coherent. One hand was on Luc's head, keeping it pressed to her breast, her fingers tangled in silky hair. The other was clenched into a fist beside her, nails digging into her palms.

Between her legs she felt sensitive and moist. As if reading her mind, Luc let his hand travel down Jesse's belly. This rang alarm bells, but Jesse didn't want to listen to alarm bells—not when her levels of desire were coiling higher and higher. Luc's wicked mouth was on her breast. Jesse said nothing. She felt him unbutton her trousers and pull the zip down. Again she said nothing.

Was she actually lifting her hips slightly, as if to tacitly tell him something her brain hadn't caught up with? When Luc's hand delved down, underneath the barrier of her knickers, Jesse stopped breathing. Everything zeroed in on his mouth and that hand. Silently she begged him to keep going. She'd never wanted anything so badly.

At that moment Luc took his mouth off her breast and

pulled back slightly. Jesse looked up at him and watched. He just looked at her while his hand moved down an inch. He was touching her curls now, threading through them with long fingers. Down another inch. Jesse's breath was back, but it was laboured. Her hand had slipped from his head and was tight around the back of his neck.

She squeezed it with the slightest pressure.

Luc said huskily, 'Is that a yes, Jesse? You want me to keep going?'

An inestimable moment passed and then Jesse squeezed again, harder this time. She barely noticed the flash of satisfaction across Luc's face because she was so intent on him touching her right...*there*. Jesse saw nothing but spots and flashes of light for a long second when Luc's fingers touched her with intimate precision.

His mouth came back over hers and, starving for him, she angled her head up to his, blindly seeking and searching for him, meeting his passion head-on with her own. Meanwhile between her legs he was stoking the raging fire within her to fever-pitch, his fingers gliding up and down, spreading her dampness, touching that most sensitive point over and over again until she had to break away and sob with frustration.

Luc looked as feverish as she felt. She felt him tugging her trousers down over her hips and, realising that this would give him more access, she raised her hips off his lap. And then he was tugging her knickers down, and her legs were free and falling open to him.

He looked down her body and said roughly, 'I want to taste you...'

Jesse didn't know what was happening until Luc shifted, so that one of her legs was over his shoulder, and he'd moved down until his head was over her belly. He pressed a kiss to her stomach, and then her belly button. She felt the rough abrasion of his tongue and squirmed against him. She knew she should be feeling vulnerable, but somehow she felt anything but.

Now his hands were on her thighs, holding them, and his mouth was descending. At the last second Jesse realised what he was doing, and the sheer carnality of it made her try to clamp her legs together.

But Luc was ruthless. He looked up at her, and his voice was guttural. 'No, let me, Jesse. Let me taste you...'

And then his breath was there, hot and...*moist*. Her head fell back. She couldn't hold it up. Her fingers were in his hair, ostensibly to stop him, but really she was holding him there, captive.

His tongue was touching her, laving her, finding all her secrets and laying her bare in a way she'd never allowed before. And then she felt his fingers parting her, exposing her, so that he could touch his tongue right to her clitoris and send her flying so close to the sun she thought she might burn to death.

One of his hands was under her buttocks, lifting her to him, and the fingers of his other hand were penetrating where she was so wet and aching, and suddenly Jesse couldn't stop the momentum. She collided with the sun and exploded into a million and one pieces. Nothing of herself was left. She was weightless and attached to the earth only by the man who was clamping her thighs apart with his big hands.

Luc was pressing kisses to her inner thigh when Jesse finally floated back down. In the aftermath of a pleasure more intense than she'd ever known could exist she became aware of the fact that one leg was still draped over Luc's shoulder and the other was wide apart. She was dressed in nothing but her shirt, which gaped open. Her breasts were pushed together because she had her hands on Luc's head, holding him to her.

And he was between her legs, looking up at her with a lazy, sexy smile and a glow of satisfaction in his eyes.

It was that which finally brought her to her senses. She

couldn't believe that one second he'd been kissing her and the next she'd been acquiescing to *anything*—until she was almost fully naked and he was between her legs. And she had to acknowledge the worst bit of it—she'd been a very *willing* participant. Begging him.

Jesse moved away from Luc so fast that she caught him unawares. She sprang up from the couch and pulled on her trousers, not even bothering with her pants. Her shirt flapped open and she scrabbled to pull it back together, but her hands were shaking too much to put buttons in holes so she just held it together with one hand.

Luc sat up, and Jesse could see with a rising sense of humiliation and abject shame that not even a button on his own shirt was askew. He was pristine—even if his hair was a little dishevelled.

'That was a mistake,' she framed shakily, aghast at how easily he'd slipped under her guard.

'It didn't sound like a mistake a few moments ago when you were screaming with pleasure.'

Jesse's humiliation rose another notch. She sensed that Luc's louche pose on the couch was anything but. She could feel the taut energy coming off him in waves. She wanted a huge hole to open up in the floor and swallow her whole. And, what was even worse, she was dangerously close to thinking about calling for a plane just to get him out of there and away from her. The only thing stopping her was the realisation that *this was exactly what he wanted*...

She struggled to hang on to her sanity. 'It was definitely a mistake, and it won't happen again. I won't let you do this... toy with me, pretend to want me...just because you think I'll give in to your demands if you seduce me.'

Jesse was shaking now, and she pointed a finger of her free hand at Luc. 'Don't think I don't know what you're up to, Luc Sanchis. All you've done is prove that I'm as humiliatingly susceptible to your overblown sexuality as the next indisciminate woman.'

'Ouch,' Luc said, and made a mock wincing face. Then his expression became much more stark and, sitting forward, elbows on his knees, he admitted, 'For your information, Jesse, a man does not do what I just did for the hell of it. He generally needs to really, *really* want to do it.'

Jesse recalled his face as he'd looked up at her and said throatily, *Let me taste you*. A fresh wave of shame washed over her. She backed away towards the entrance to the room. Luc stood up and her panic rose. If he touched her again… Her mind blanked at the prospect.

'No. It was a mistake. I won't be so weak again.'

And with that she turned and fled, bare feet slapping across the floor of the hall and then up the stairs to her room, two stairs at a time. She heard Luc curse behind her, and then she could hear his footsteps. Panic galvanised her and she got into her room and closed the door just as his hand connected with it.

'Go away!' Jesse shouted.

But Luc opened the door and pushed. Jesse couldn't hold it and sprang back into the room. Luc stood there like some marauding pirate of old, dominating the doorway. She was still clutching her shirt. A treacherous lick of excitement curled through Jesse's abdomen.

It shook her so much she said, 'Get away from me, you… *animal*! You don't want me any more than you want a block of wood and you're only trying to mess with my head. I won't let it happen again.'

Luc emitted a sound like a growl and crossed the room to Jesse. He grabbed her hand and placed it roughly onto a very *hard* part of his anatomy. She could feel the blood rushing to heat her face—which was ridiculous when she thought of what he'd just been doing to her.

He felt massive.

He pressed her hand even closer. 'Do you think I can just conjure that response up? Do you really think that's the sign of a man who is disengaged with what he's doing? I don't know where you did your biology classes, but I can assure you it's not.'

She was stunned to recognise that he was angrier than she'd ever seen him before. With that he flung her hand away and strode back to the door, leaving Jesse standing there tingling all over and with a dull, throbbing ache between her legs.

He stopped abruptly by the door and Jesse heard something clink, like metal against metal, and then he turned around to face her again. She couldn't make out his expression, because he was in shadow, but she could see what he was holding up in his hand. It glinted in the low lamplight: the key from the door.

Instantly she went clammy all over. He wouldn't...

'Let's see how *you* like being a prisoner for a while, Jesse. I think that's only fair, don't you?'

Then he was gone, and the door was shut, and Jesse heard the key turn in the lock. And her world disintegrated around her.

Luc went downstairs, borne aloft by the rage thrumming through his blood. All he could see was red, and he cursed his own rampant body which was refusing to cool down. What did he think he was doing? All but stripping Jesse completely and making love to her on the couch like some horny, out-of-control teenager?

Luc was used to sophisticated surroundings and sophisticated women. He was used to a certain controllable level of arousal which never became something so blindingly white-hot and intense that he forgot who he was and where he was.

And that was the problem.

He stood in the centre of the living room and funnelled his fingers through his hair. He'd never lost it like that. Not even with Maria. He scowled, hating how comparisons between Jesse and Maria kept popping into his head, as if to flag up to him that this whole situation was ten times more volatile.

He'd set out to seduce Jesse, yes. He'd set out to unsettle her, and perhaps to encourage her to trust him by making her vulnerable to him.

He saw her in his mind's eye as she'd stood there clasping her shirt, spitting mad. He wasn't making her vulnerable at all. He was making her even harder to win around. So much for his famed charm.

Luc cursed.

He strode into the kitchen and saw Tigger's box. He hoped that by tending to the kitten for a few minutes it might calm him down. But the delicacy of the tiny animal in his hands only served to remind him of how delicate Jesse had felt under his hands. *Damn, damn, damn.*

Luc went back to the living room and found the drinks cabinet and poured himself a healthy shot of the finest Irish whiskey. Mentally apologising to the absent owner, he downed it in one.

The fact was his extreme response to kissing Jesse and how fast things had escalated out of control unsettled him. It had manifested as anger at *her*, but now he could see that it was entirely directed at himself.

Luc took another healthy swig of whiskey before putting the bottle back. He thought of Jesse, upstairs stewing, too stubborn to ask to be let out of her room, and felt a wry grin tugging at his mouth. And just as quickly that insidious heat he felt whenever he thought of her crept back into his body, firing his blood all over again.

Luc sighed deeply and then went towards the stairs. Time

to repair the damage and try to keep his hands off Jesse long enough to make her believe that he had at least an ounce of civility in him—although he couldn't imagine anything he wanted more than to strip her bare completely and lock them *both* in a room for the forseeable future.

Outside her door he couldn't hear a sound. He knocked lightly. 'Jesse?'

Nothing.

Something like foreboding trickled down Luc's spine and he turned the key in the lock and opened the door. The room was exactly as he'd left it, and at first he couldn't see Jesse, but once his eyes adjusted to the dim light he saw her: she was huddled with her knees up to her chest and her arms wrapped around them in a corner of the room.

Something about her form told him that this was not her sulking. He walked over and crouched down in front of her. 'Jesse? What…?'

Her head was down on her knees, and Luc saw then that she was trembling all over. He sat and slid along the wall beside her, put his arm around her, tugging her stiff body to him. Something was terribly wrong.

'Jesse, what is it? What happened?'

Her voice was muffled and she was out of breath. 'Locked in…can't get out…need help…'

Luc cursed his impetuosity. Carefully he tried to take Jesse's arms from around her legs and put a hand under her jaw. His stomach clenched when he felt the unmistakable moisture of tears on her face.

She wouldn't or couldn't look at him. Her eyes seemed to be sightless. He recognised shock.

'Jesse, you're not locked in any more. The door is open. You're here with me, Luc. It's okay. I'm sorry. I shouldn't have locked you in.'

Jesse was shaking her head, the trembling in her body increasing. 'No…you don't understand. It's my mother. She's *dead*. She's died and I can't get out to tell anyone. He doesn't believe me. I need to get help; I need to get *out*.'

Luc put his hands around Jesse's face and turned it so she had to look at him. 'Jesse, it's me. Only me. Just the two of us. Your mother isn't here.'

'No,' Jesse said brokenly, 'because she's *dead*. He killed her, let her die.'

Luc shook his head, trying to make sense of what she said. 'Who killed her, Jesse?'

'My father.'

Her voice scared him. It was so hard and flat.

Luc faintly remembered her saying that she didn't know who her father was but clearly she *did*. He could feel her trembling turn into a violent shaking. Locking her into the room had obviously sent her back to some trauma in her life.

Luc cursed out loud, but Jesse was oblivious.

In one move, he stood and lifted her into his arms. He walked them both into the bathroom and put Jesse down for a moment, securing her limp body against him while he reached into the shower to turn it on. Soon steam was filling the room. He looked down at Jesse and saw how pale she was. He cursed again.

Without waiting, Luc put them both under the shower, and once under the powerful hot spray started to take off Jesse's clothes and then his own. His heart ached in a peculiar way when he saw she was as unresisting as a child. When they were both naked he pulled her to him and wrapped his arms around her, willing his body heat into her, stroking her head and back, saying nonsensical things.

He felt the moment she began to come back to herself. Tension came into her body—but a different kind of tension. She started to move, and Luc had to grit his jaw against the inevitable response in his own body. He was already as hard as a rock, and trying to angle himself in such a way so as not to draw attention to that fact.

He pulled back and looked down at Jesse. She was blinking up into his face, and a sigh of relief moved through him at the sight of colour in her cheeks again. He tried valiantly to block out the view of water running in rivulets over her pert breasts.

Reaching out, he snagged a robe and then turned off the water. He wrapped the robe around Jesse, rubbing up and down her arms and back briskly.

He stopped for a moment and looked at her. 'Are you okay?'

# CHAPTER EIGHT

JESSE looked up into Luc's eyes. She had complete recollection of what had just happened, but it was as if it had happened to someone else. And in a way it had: to her child self.

Belatedly answering Luc's question, she nodded abruptly. She was suddenly far too aware that she was standing in a steamy shower with a very naked Luc Sanchis. Praying that her legs would support her, she turned and stepped out of his hands into the bathroom, noticing their sodden clothes on the ground.

She found the holes for her arms in the robe and put them in, tying the belt securely around her. She felt raw, as if she'd been flayed. She heard Luc moving behind her and went into the bedroom to sit on the end of the bed. He was standing in the doorway to the bathroom with a towel around his hips. The light behind him was throwing his broad build into sharp relief, and Jesse felt that ever-present awareness curl into her belly.

He leant against the door and crossed his arms. 'Do you want to explain what just happened?'

Jesse gulped and looked away. The strength of her reaction to being locked into the room scared her. She knew she'd always had a thing about it, but somehow here her past was reaching up to grip her around the neck with an ease that terrified her. She felt a strong urge to articulate it—as if she knew that it might be the only way to stop it happening again.

She glanced back to Luc and saw the lines of his face, intent and serious. She looked down at her lap and plucked at a stray thread.

'When I was nine I was locked into a room with my mother for a night. She was sick, and during the night she died... I couldn't get out. No one could hear me. I was with her dead body until someone finally opened the door the next day.'

'Hell...'

She heard Luc moving, the muffled sound of a chair being moved across the floor, and then he was sitting in front of her, taking her hands. Reluctantly she looked at him, and the expression on his face made her feel a swooping sensation in her belly.

'How on earth could something like that happen?'

Jesse grimaced. 'I knew she was very ill. She'd been sick for days but hadn't gone to the doctor... I went to get help, but he wouldn't listen to me.'

'You mentioned your father just now... Was it your father you asked for help?'

Jesse nodded. She felt numb inside. 'He was hosting a dinner party that night. He was drunk and didn't want to be disturbed. He took me back to the bedroom and told me to stop bothering him. When I went after him again he locked me in...'

Jesse remembered her father lurching unsteadily over to her mother in the bed and feeling her clammy forehead before declaring, 'She's fine. It's just a cold.'

She looked at Luc, needing to erase that memory of her father.

'By the time morning came and someone opened the door she was dead—had been for hours...'

Luc frowned. 'Where was your father?'

Jesse shrugged. 'At work…'

Luc frowned, and then he said, 'But earlier you locked the door to the study…'

Jesse blushed. 'I just pretended to lock it.'

Luc's mouth tipped up wryly. 'I didn't even think to test it.'

Something infinitely delicate seemed to stretch between them at that moment.

Luc gripped Jesse's hands tighter. 'I'm sorry for locking you in. If I'd had any idea—'

Jesse put her hand over his mouth, and took it away again quickly when his warm breath feathered against her palm. 'You weren't to know. *I* didn't know I'd react like that.' She ducked her head. 'It's embarrassing.'

Luc tipped up her chin and looked at her. 'No, it's not embarrassing. Your father was a monster, Jesse, to do that to you and your mother.'

'Yes, he was.'

'Is that why you told me you didn't know who your father was? Because you don't like to talk about him?'

Jesse felt guilty. 'Something like that.'

To her surprise Luc stood up, and Jesse blushed when she registered what part of his anatomy her eyes were on a level with.

He stepped back and said lightly, 'You must be tired. You should get some rest.'

Jesse stood up too, some of those tendrils of icy panic reaching out for her again at the prospect of Luc walking out. Without thinking she put out a hand, curling it around his wrist. It felt vital and alive beneath her palm. His pulse was strong and powerful. She suddenly knew that she needed this, needed him, as she'd never needed anything before in her life. Right in that moment she trusted him implicitly.

Huskily she said, 'Please don't leave me alone.'

He stopped and turned to face her directly. 'What are you saying, Jesse?'

She looked up at him, feeling as if she was stepping out into a void. 'Please stay with me tonight.'

Jesse could see Luc's jaw clench.

Carefully he said, 'If I stay with you we share a bed, and if we share a bed we won't be doing much sleeping.'

Wild excitement rushed through her, obliterating the awful memories and the fear that had gripped her. She stepped closer to Luc, his wrist still in her hand. 'That's what I was hoping you'd say...'

In some dim and distant recess of her mind Jesse couldn't believe she was being so forward, but for the first time in her life everything felt *right*. This man, this moment. The past few days, everything that had happened, the way he'd reacted just now and the moments when he'd shown her real gentleness—she had come to trust him on some very deep and vulnerable level, but she couldn't really acknowledge that now. She could only act on it.

Luc said, 'Are you sure?'

Jesse just said, 'Stop talking, Sanchis...' and dropped his wrist. She reached up and put her arms around his neck, funnelled her hands through his hair, urging his head down to hers. 'Kiss me.'

Luc's arms went around her waist, dragging her even closer. Jesse could feel the thrilling hard ridge of his arousal and moved against him.

He growled softly. 'I thought I told you we've gone way beyond such formality...'

He lowered his head and pulled her up to meet him. Their mouths met and Jesse melted into a sea of raging hormones. They kissed for what felt like for ever, tongues tangling together in a languorous erotic dance. And then Jesse felt herself being lowered onto her bed. She lay back and looked up at Luc, eyes drinking in his hard-boned form greedily.

He came down over her on his arms, not even touching her yet, tantalising her. Emboldened, Jesse moved her hands to her robe and undid the knot. She pulled the robe open and saw Luc's eyes widen and flash with fire as his gaze dipped and dwelled on all her secrets and hollows.

Impatient, Jesse came up slightly and reached for his towel, tugging so that it came apart and fell to the floor. Her own eyes widened when she took in the sheer male perfection of his body. She'd seen him naked already, but she hadn't seen him naked and aroused.

A little overwhelmed, she fell back onto the bed, unaware that her legs were parting instinctively. Luc smiled, and it was feral. He stroked a hand down Jesse's body, over her collarbone and over one tip-tilted breast, dwelling there to squeeze her nipple gently, making her gasp. And then his hand continued to the cleft between her legs.

His fingers found where she was moist and aching. Jesse moved her hips against him. 'Luc…please.'

Luc's fingers moved against her, teasing her. Biting her lip, Jesse moved so that she could reach him and wrap one hand around his hard girth. She exulted in his own deeply drawn breath.

'You're playing with fire now…'

Jesse felt urgency building and stroked her hand up and down his shaft, wanting him to fill her. She tried to draw him closer, every muscle in her body crying out when she held the tip of him at her entrance.

A wave of sensation was already rolling through Jesse's body. And, as if she'd finally pushed him too far, Luc gently prised her hand from him and balanced on his hands over her, then thrust deep into her clasping body.

Jesse was so ready and sensitised that she convulsed

around Luc immediately, countless waves of pleasure holding her suspended before diminishing and leaving her breathless. She felt the sweat on her skin, and tremors racked her body.

Embarrassed at the strength of her reaction, she ducked her head into Luc's shoulder. 'I'm sorry...'

He tipped up her chin. 'Never be sorry for being so responsive.'

Jesse felt intensely gauche. 'But I... You haven't even...'

'No,' he agreed in thrillingly deep tones. 'But I fully intend to.'

And with that he started to move slowly, in and out. Jesse was over-sensitive for a second, but then her body started to adjust and she could feel that urgency building all over again. She gripped his arms with her hands and wrapped her legs around his back, feeling him slide even deeper.

Soon Luc's movements became harder and faster, and Jesse could feel herself climbing. She only half heard Luc's guttural-sounding, *'Damn...'* She was too intent on reaching that pinnacle of pleasure again.

And then she saw the tortured expression on his face. 'What is it?'

Luc gritted out painfully, 'No protection...'

But they were both too far gone. Jesse could feel her muscles start to clamp around him, urging him to completion. Luc threw his head back and shouted out, and at the last second, when everything in Jesse broke free of the delicious tension and soared even higher than before, Luc pulled free of her body and twisted away from her.

Despite the intensity of her climax Jesse felt bereft, as if she'd been cheated of something. She lay there panting, the sweat cooling on her body, and became aware that her arms weren't even fully out of the robe. She shrugged out of it now and instinctively curled into Luc's back. She tucked her legs under his, breathed his scent in deep and welcomed a sweet oblivion she'd never tasted before.

Luc lay for a long time, staring into the middle distance as his body came down from the mind-bending crescendo it had just experienced. Jesse's arm was around him like a vice and, contrary to what was usual for him, his first impulse wasn't to get out of her embrace. Instead he found his hand coming up to hold hers against him.

He felt as if he'd just been turned inside out. He'd never, *ever* forgotten about protection before, was far too wary of unplanned pregnancies, and yet it had been the last thing on his mind right up until it had been too late. The only option left to him had been to withdraw and spill himself on the bed like a callow youth. For the *second* time that evening he'd been reduced to baser tendencies than he was used to.

But what was even more disconcerting was how right it had felt to thrust into Jesse's tight, slick heat skin-to-skin, and how hard it had been to pull free as his climax had approached, robbing him of any remaining sanity. Even now he couldn't be sure that they'd been entirely safe…

Luc shifted onto his back and Jesse snuggled sleepily into his chest, one leg coming up to rest over his thigh—disturbingly close to a far too sensitive part of his anatomy. The arm across his chest tightened. Her breasts pressed against his side. And Luc sighed deeply as the resurgence of desire rushed through his body…

What had happened in this room this evening posed far too many intriguing questions. The ease with which Luc had imagined rattling Jesse's cage was almost laughable now. She was the one rattling *his* cage, and he didn't like it one bit.

'I thought I wasn't any good at…sex.'

Jesse blushed against Luc's chest. What on earth had made

her blurt that out? She felt Luc move, and then she was on her back and he was looming over her, looking deliciously tousled and with a dark shadow on his jaw.

They'd been in bed all day and most of the evening, after a brief hiatus at about seven that morning, when Luc had summarily carried her down to the kitchen for a delicious breakfast. By some unspoken agreement they'd spoken of nothing controversial—nothing beyond the island—to link to harsh reality. It was as if they'd silently mutually decided to embark on a tenuous truce.

'Well, I can assert that you are *very* good at sex.'

Jesse blushed more now, and put her hands to her face.

Luc took them and pinned them over her head with one hand, before resting his other hand near the apex of her legs. It had an immediate effect on her breathing, and not for the first time in the last twenty-four hours did she welcome physical release over the clamour of voices in her head, urging her to stop and think about what was happening between them…

'Whoever gave you the idea that you weren't?'

Jesse squirmed, hating that the fact Luc was holding her hands captive sent such thrills of excitement through her body. 'I was involved with someone briefly a few years ago. I tried to like it…but when he touched me I just felt cold inside. And yet with you I felt hot the first time you looked at me.'

Luc said, 'Do you remember bumping into me at that function?'

Jesse nodded and bit her lip. She felt vulnerable now, remembering the way he'd thrust her away from him that night. Sudden doubt assailed her. The cacophony of inner voices became louder. Perhaps this was all part of his plan and even now he was playing her…pretending to desire her…forcing his body to respond.

'I wanted you then.'

Jesse blurted out, 'But you pushed me away from you…'

Luc grimaced, his hand tightening on hers fractionally. His other hand was touching the curls covering her sex. 'I'd been watching you…wondering about you…'

All Jesse's doubts melted away like traitors. 'You had?'

He nodded. 'And then you walked straight into my arms and looked up at me…and seemed to see right into me.'

Jesse felt scary emotion grip her. 'That's what I felt too…'

He bent his head to kiss her just as his hand reached for that sweet spot between her legs and Jesse's back arched. She let emotion and doubt be swallowed up in the heat which rose around them again.

When Luc broke off the kiss he commanded her with a rough voice, '*Don't* take your hands down or I'll tie them there.'

Jesse felt the illicit burn of excitement and curled her fingers around the bed's headboard. Luc made his way down her body, teasing every inch of her with a thoroughness that had her writhing and aching and begging for release. Until he got between her legs, when his breath and mouth sent her soaring up into the light where she couldn't speak any more.

When Luc entered her with a cataclysmic thrust Jesse took down her hands, uncaring of his threat, because she had to touch him or die. She shut her eyes and rose up to meet the bliss Luc promised her, ignoring those insidious voices, whispering that she was heading for certain catastrophe.

'So, tell me how you really learnt to cook.'

Jesse was sitting on a stool with her chin propped in her hand, watching Luc do something very complicated to a fish in a pan. She'd drunk half a glass of wine and felt incredibly mellow. Which most likely also had a lot to do with the fact that this was the evening after their whole day in bed. A bone-deep sense of satisfaction oozed through Jesse's entire body.

Luc's voice was light, but she sensed an undercurrent of

steel—as if she was touching on a tender point. 'I told you—my mother had a breakdown after my father died and I had to cook for me and my sister and her when she came out of hospital.'

Impetuously Jesse asked, 'How did your father die?'

Luc's jaw tightened. He drizzled some oil over the fish in the pan and it sizzled.

When he said casually, 'He killed himself,' Jesse almost missed it. Before she could say anything Luc was explaining, 'I told you that my sister has special needs? That she's verging on autistic?'

Jesse nodded, knowing well enough not to mention his father again. Her heart ached for Luc in a very peculiar way, but her mind skittered weakly away from looking at *why* too closely. Much as it skittered away from analysing anything of the last couple of days too deeply.

Luc went on. 'I discovered that cooking calmed her. Getting the ingredients and putting them together seemed to occupy her.' He grimaced. 'Of course when things didn't work out as they should she would fly into a rage, but that just made it more imperative that I learn how to do things properly. The more complicated the recipe, the more it would have an effect on her. She would sit for hours and watch a *boeuf bourguignon* cooking slowly.'

He looked at Jesse and smiled faintly. 'She's now working as a chef for a company that caters for people with special needs. It's like meals on wheels, and they offer opportunities to people like Eva.'

Jesse's voice was husky. 'Eva is a pretty name.'

Then Luc asked, 'So, what happened after your mother died?'

Jesse blanched and took a hasty sip of wine. She almost resented Luc for skirting so close to dangerous reality.

Very reluctantly she said, 'I was taken in by the Social Services… I lived in foster homes until I was eighteen.'

Luc looked at her. 'That must have been rough.'

Jesse shrugged and avoided his eye. 'It wasn't easy.'

'But what about your father? Why didn't you live with him—despite what he did?'

Jesse realised that Luc must have assumed that her mother and father had been married. The old shame crawled up her spine. 'My parents weren't married… My mother was my father's housekeeper.' Her mouth twisted with bitterness as she revealed, '*He* was married to a very honourable woman from English society.'

Luc's hands stilled. 'So…your mother and father had an affair and you were brought up in the house?'

'More or less…except it wasn't so much an affair as my father using my mother whenever he felt like it.'

Luc's voice was cold. 'He *knew* he was your father?'

Jesse nodded and finally looked at him again, not sure how she felt at seeing the condemnation in his eyes.

Before she knew it the words were tumbling out. 'I went to him one day when he was in his study… I don't know where I got the nerve… I must have been about six. I was going through a phase where I was missing not having a daddy. And I knew he was my father. So I went and asked him why he didn't act like the fathers I saw at school…'

'Jesse—'

But she held up a hand, stopping Luc in whatever he was going to say, and finished. 'He said nothing at first. He just got up and went and closed and locked the door to his study. And then he took off his belt. He whipped me with it, all down my back and legs, until there was blood on the floor. The buckle broke my skin…'

Luc had left the fish and come round to stand in front of

Jesse. When he cupped her face in his hands and lifted it up she was surprised to feel tears running down her face.

'He told me never, ever to call him my father again, and that if I repeated what I'd said to anyone he'd kill me and my mother.'

Luc shook his head. 'No wonder you have a thing about locked rooms. Was he violent to your mother?'

Jesse nodded. She felt Luc gather her into his chest and rock her. He felt so solid and strong and warm. Her hands gripped his shirt, holding on tight until she was still.

When he let her go and gave her a tissue she hiccuped. 'I'm sorry, I've never told anyone about that before... I don't usually cry.'

'Don't be sorry. Is he still—?'

Jesse stopped his words by blurting out, 'Please—I don't want to talk about it any more, okay?'

After dinner, and much later that night in bed, Luc asked softly, 'Those scars on your legs...are they from that day?'

Jesse came up on one arm and looked at Luc. She just nodded. And then, to stop him asking any more questions, she bent down and kissed him on the mouth, slid over him so that her thighs were straddling his hips and her breasts were crushed into his chest.

Luc clamped his hands around her hips and lifted her slightly until she felt him guiding his erection between her legs. And Jesse weakly obliterated everything from her mind except this exquisite moment.

When the storm had passed Jesse curled into Luc's side, once again claiming him in sleep in a way which should have had him prising her from him, but which was having the opposite effect.

Luc felt more than a little pole-axed. When Jesse had told him about her father earlier a tidal wave of anger had come over him at the thought of her being so abused. And also a feeling of pride…that she'd come through something like that and forged such a successful life for herself.

He sighed deeply and recognised that he was in serious danger of becoming so sidelined by this woman that he'd forget about his primary focus, which was to get off the island and get back in time to deal with O'Brien.

He had Jesse exactly where he wanted her—*literally*—but he found that instead of exploiting this intimacy he was intent on seducing her some more…and then some more. She was a fever in his blood, and he was very much afraid he wasn't ready to douse it just yet.

Luc felt the old tentacles of vulnerability reach out to touch him with ghostly memories, but he pushed them aside and damned them all. Jesse was different…this situation was different. He would never be led astray again.

As he fell asleep he reassured himself that he hadn't lost sight of his goal at all. He was still entirely focused on his endgame, and in complete control of what was happening…

Jesse was sitting on the couch in the den, feeling more sated than she'd ever felt in her life. After waking late, and a lazy, lingering brunch, which had inevitably ended with them back in bed, she'd left Luc asleep upstairs to come down and see to Tigger. Before she'd left the bedroom, though, she'd spent an indulgent moment watching Luc, his big body sprawled in abandon, utterly self-confident even in sleep.

She watched Tigger now, who was valiantly trying to unthread the stunning oriental carpet on the floor with his tiny claws, and deftly lifted him out of harm's way and onto the couch beside her. He promptly went to the edge and looked down the great distance. He miaowed indignantly, and she smiled at his clear frustration.

She lifted him up and took him into the kitchen saying into his sweet fur, 'I think it's milk and nap time for baby cats…'

It was only when she was tucking him into his box and watching him lap greedily at the milk that Jesse realised with a shock just how far into a fantasy world she'd allowed herself to travel.

In the past few days, since everything had become physical between her and Luc, she had somehow begun to imagine that perhaps this was real. That this bubble was not some mad aberration. When the reality was that she'd kidnapped Luc Sanchis to stop him from saving her father...which he must still want to do at all costs. She'd conveniently blocked that out because she'd become far more interested in the physical nirvana Luc promised every time he touched her.

She heard him call her name now, faintly, from upstairs. Galvanised by panic, because she couldn't have him look at her with that far too perceptive gaze when she felt so exposed, Jesse lurched out of the villa and down a path she hadn't yet explored. It led to a beautifully soft and sandy private cove. But Jesse was oblivious.

She hugged her arms around herself at the water's edge, feeling cold. What had she been thinking, allowing Luc to seduce her like this? She mocked herself. More accurately, what had she been thinking, allowing herself to be a full and willing participant in that seduction?

The deadline was in three days' time. Three days and her father would be ruined. She'd almost lost sight of that goal. If Luc had turned to her that morning as they'd lain in his bed and said to her, *I really need to get back to work...* Jesse would most likely have tripped downstairs and rung for a jet before she'd even realised what she was doing.

With a little sob of emotion that made her clamp her hand over her mouth, she realised *I don't know who I am any more!* The cool shell she'd built up to keep people at arm's length was well and truly gone. She'd turned into someone who cried at the drop of a hat and was happy to blurt out secrets she'd harboured for a lifetime. Not even the nicest of her social workers or foster parents had managed to get her to reveal what had happened to her, and yet with Luc she'd spilled it all.

How could she trust anything that had happened between them? She imagined Luc waking and remembering with distaste that he had a job to do: to try to make Jesse believe he really wanted her. This whole environment was contrived and false. From the moment she'd forced Luc onto this island she shouldn't have trusted anything. Or him. No matter how much the weak part of her believed she could or longed to.

She'd seen how her father had charmed people when she was small—only to turn around and stab them in the back with cruel words as soon as they'd gone. And now she knew worse than that: her father had ruined the businesses of people who'd slighted him over dinner. So she knew how easily someone could present a façade when it suited them…

Luc's words came back to her—words he'd said only days ago: *All you've done is make yourself a foe for life… I will find out all your secrets and you will pay…*

After long minutes of looking blankly at the sea, feeling as if a part of her soul was ebbing away, Jesse went back inside. She found Luc in the den, and valiantly ignored the kick of her heart when she saw him.

He turned from where he'd been looking out at the view, with his hands in the pockets of his trousers. His hair was damp from the shower. Incredible pain lanced Jesse, but she ignored that too.

He said to her now, 'That storm never did materialise, did it?'

Jesse shook her head. Not that storm. But another storm had. It had whipped her up inside so intensely that she knew she'd never emerge as the same person.

Luc squared his body to face her more fully, and Jesse had

the uncanny prescience that she wasn't the only one who'd just faced some revelations.

'Your name…Moriarty…it's Irish, isn't it?'

Jesse nodded, a little blindsided by this observation. 'Yes, it is… My mother was Irish—from Kerry.'

'O'Brien is Irish too…'

Jesse went cold all over. Goosebumps broke out on her skin. And then Luc said it out loud.

'He's your father, isn't he, Jesse? Your mother was his housekeeper.'

# CHAPTER NINE

*'HE's your father, isn't he, Jesse? Your mother was his house-keeper.'*

Luc must have seen the instantaneous reaction of shock on Jesse's face, because he obviously took it as confirmation.

He continued, seemingly unaware of the seismic reaction within Jesse. 'What I'd like to know is, after everything he's done to you, why the hell do you want to save him?'

For a second she thought she might faint. As if sensing it, Luc crossed the distance between them and took her arm; he led her to the couch where he forced her to sit down.

He glared down at her, hands on his hips. 'Why didn't you tell me this from the start?'

Jesse felt far too vulnerable where she was, so she scrambled off the couch and went to stand apart from Luc, crossing her arms. 'I didn't tell you because it has no relevance to anything.'

Even Jesse winced at those words, and she flinched slightly at Luc's caustic laugh.

'Give me a break, Jesse. It has *everything* to do with this. Why else would you want to save him so badly? Clearly you have some misguided sense of loyalty to the man—'

*'No!'* Jesse reacted viscerally to those words, cutting Luc off. 'I don't want to save him.'

He looked at her. 'Excuse me?'

Jesse swallowed. 'I don't want to save him. I want to ruin him. I want him to be finished for ever. And I'm not going to let you be the one to save him. That's why I wanted to buy you out—so that no one else would come to his aid...'

For a long tense moment they stared at each other across the divide, and then inexplicably Luc threw back his head and laughed. Jesse just stared at him. But he kept laughing. He couldn't seem to stop. Eventually he had to sit down on the couch. Tears were running from his eyes.

Anger was rushing upwards inside Jesse; she'd completely exposed herself and he was *laughing* at her.

She stalked over to Luc and stood over him, much as he'd just done to her. 'What's so funny about that?'

Luc stood up, sober now, making her move back. He shook his head. 'What's so funny about it, Jesse—what's so ridiculous—is that all this time we've been on the same side...'

'What do you mean?' Jesse asked faintly.

She found herself wanting to believe Luc so badly. But at that moment he turned away from her and ran his hands through his hair. She couldn't see his expression, and in the few seconds before he turned back to face her she remembered standing on that small beach just now. She had the stark realisation that no matter what Luc said now she couldn't trust him fully. She had to remember that or it could all still unravel.

'What I mean,' Luc said, when he turned back, 'is that I want to see him gone too. I was going to wait until the last moment—until I knew no one else could step in to help him—and then walk away from the deal.'

'What?'

'When I told you I was interested in his Eastern European concerns it was the truth—but only insofar as I have every intention of saving them for myself and letting him go to hell with the rest of his poisoned businesses. Not that he's aware of that... *yet*.'

Jesse looked at him and fought down the trembling flame of hope inside her. She had to be strong. She'd prepared for this her whole life.

She paced away from Luc with crossed arms, and then turned back to face him. 'What possible motive could you have for wanting to see him ruined?'

She tried not to notice how vibrant and gorgeous he looked in the dying light of the sun as it streamed in the huge windows. She tried to stop her heart from thumping just a little too hard.

'I told you that my father killed himself.'

Jesse nodded.

Luc paced back and forth, taut energy radiating out from his body. 'My father was a construction foreman for a company owned by your father in Malaga. One day there was a terrible accident and my father was badly injured. He had to have both legs amputated from the knees down.' Luc shook his head. 'When he came home he was a shell of his former self. He was so ashamed of what had happened even though it wasn't even his fault. It was outdated machinery.'

Luc slashed a hand down. 'Of course there was little or no health and safety regulations in those days, and as for litigation or admission of culpability…' He sneered. 'O'Brien merely hired a new foreman and got on with his work. It was only when the next person had a fatal accident that he was forced to close the plant down.'

'What happened?' she asked quietly.

Luc looked at her now and she shivered. His eyes were so black.

'My father couldn't cope with being less than a full man. He'd been very proud. My mother was barely coping too, and Eva…she was so young at the time, and difficult. One night I woke up because my mother was screaming. I rushed outside and my father was sitting in his car, in the garage, with the engine on. It was too late to save him.'

Jesse clenched her arms tighter. 'I'm sorry, Luc.'

'Yes,' he said flatly, 'I'm sorry too. I went to see your father once, when I knew he was visiting the factory one day. It was before my father died. I went to beg him for help. He did exactly the same thing to me, Jesse. He took me into his office and locked the door...'

He gave a curt laugh. 'Not once since we met again has he even remembered the name of Sanchis—or me as that young boy who confronted him.'

Jesse knew her father had been behind plenty of dodgy practices over the years. Dozens of claims had been mounted against him, but all had come to nothing because he was so well protected. Why would he remember the son of one man from one of his many factories dotted around Europe?

Everything urged her to believe Luc, but she felt as if she was being torn in two. She could feel emotion rising, and she wanted to tell Luc to stop—but he wouldn't. It was as if he was binding her tighter and tighter with his words and soon she wouldn't be able to walk away... Her heart was too soft. This was when she had to be most vigilant. But it was agony.

'He told me that if I ever came back saying anything about my father he'd hurt my mother and Eva. He didn't touch me physically, but he didn't have to.'

Jesse was shaking her head now, her vision blurring. 'No. Stop it. You're making it up. You've gone too far, Luc. I won't stand here and listen to you trick me into believing something like this. It's too coincidental.'

She turned to rush from the room, but Luc caught her and whirled her around in his arms. 'Damn it, Jesse, I'm not lying. It's all true.'

Jesse dashed her tears aside. Suddenly she longed for the

cool, emotionless austerity of her life before she'd met this man. 'Can you prove it?'

The expression on Luc's face was fearsome, and his hands tightened on her arms. 'My father was foreman of a lowly construction company in southern Spain. Do you really think it made the papers?' His mouth twisted when he added, 'And yet despite that it managed to wreck a whole family.'

Jesse looked up at Luc. She could already feel that intensity reaching out to ensnare her. She was so susceptible to this man.

She pulled out of his arms with effort, and finally he let her go. She backed away from him and shook her head. 'I'm sorry. I just need to be alone for a while…'

Luc battled the urge to grab Jesse back to him, clenching his fists at his sides and watching her slim back retreat. It was a lot to take in, and more than a little fantastical to discover that they'd both had the same objective all along.

When he'd woken in the bed earlier, to find Jesse gone, it had been as if his brain had been working overtime during sleep. He'd had a dream of Jesse and her father, a faceless threatening presence locking her into a room, and just like that Luc had *known*. The links were too many to dismiss. Why on earth would someone like her be interested in someone like O'Brien unless it was for some personal reason? He just hadn't figured that it was for the opposite reason he'd initially suspected.

Luc had so many more questions, but Jesse's face before she'd left the room, stark with shock and emotion, made him cautious. He'd have to give her some time. But surely now there could be no objection to their returning to England together?

When he thought of that his heart gave an involuntary kick, and for the first time in years Luc knew he was on very shaky ground.

* * *

Later that night Luc woke abruptly when he heard a sound that was familiar but *un*familiar, because he'd got so used to the peace and quiet of the island.

He hadn't seen Jesse again that evening. She'd stayed holed up in her room and Luc had decided to give her more time, resisting his urge to batter the door down and kiss her into trusting him.

He looked at his watch and saw he'd only been asleep for a couple of hours. And then the sound registered fully: *helicopter.*

He jumped out of bed, pulling on his boxer shorts, and silently thanked Jesse for coming to her senses. He half expected to bump into her when he opened his bedroom door, but the villa was silent. An awful slither of foreboding went down his spine.

He went downstairs and could still hear the unmistakable *thwop-thwop* of the helicopter. And then he saw the note, and a phone on the hall table. He went over and picked up the piece of paper:

*Dear Luc*
*The phone only accepts incoming calls. If your mother or sister need you they'll call me and I'll let you know. I can't trust that if they call you, you won't try to get off the island before Friday.*

*At one p.m. on Friday someone will arrive to take you to the landing strip, where a plane will be waiting with all your possessions. The pilot will take you wherever you want to go.*

*I'm so sorry.*

*I hope you can understand why I need to do this.*
*Jesse.*

With an inarticulate roar of pure rage Luc stormed over to the villa door and opened it just in time to see the flashing lights of the helicopter as it rose up into the night sky, banked to the right and then disappeared into the distance.

For long seconds, as the island fell into silence again, Luc couldn't believe what had just happened. And then it became painfully crystal-clear. Once again a woman had taken his trust and betrayed him—except this time it was far, far worse.

High above the black expanse of sea Jesse sat in the helicopter with tears running down her face. *Why couldn't she stop crying?* She struggled to control herself, glad of the sound of the engine and the blades which precluded any conversation. In her lap she held the squirmy bundle which was Tigger, and she stroked him absently, trying to keep him calm.

She'd had to leave because she knew she couldn't last two more days in that villa alone with Luc. Couldn't trust that he wouldn't use everything he now knew about her to wear her down and make her trust him…make her believe him… when he could still turn around and rip her world from under her feet.

Earlier she'd been so close to trusting him, believing him, but how could she? How could she trust him after only a few days spent together? No matter how intimate they'd been?

*Trust.* It was the one thing she'd never been able to do with anyone after her trust had been so comprehensively eroded at an early age, and then over and over again as she'd grown up.

She had to be strong and remember that Luc's prime motivation all along had been to get off the island, whether it was for the same reasons as Jesse or not. That was why he'd seduced her in the first place.

Pain, swift and agonising, rose up to clench Jesse's heart.

She'd *wanted* to trust him so badly. The first time she'd wanted it in her life. And that was when she'd finally had to heed the danger of her situation. If she trusted Luc then she'd learnt nothing. All her years of struggle to prevail would have been for naught.

She simply had to shut down her mind and forget about what had happened. It was a mirage. It had never really existed. Because would someone like Luc ever have *really* seduced her if given a choice? She went cold. Of course not.

She knew he'd never forgive her for this.

Jesse closed her eyes on the starry sky outside and shut down inside. She retreated back to a place she knew, where she was icy and removed from anything too painful.

When she finally got to Britain, on the plane that had been waiting for her in Athens, the woman at Immigration said officiously, 'You need a licence for that animal—he needs to be checked and given shots and registered.'

Jesse shook her head, the thought of being separated from Tigger breaking through the ice. 'I didn't realise. I've never owned a pet before...'

The immigration official looked from Jesse's red eyes and puffy face to the tiny ball of fur miaowing pathetically occasionally. She sighed and looked at her watch. It was four a.m., and Jesse was the only passenger.

'I could lose my job for this, but I'm going to pretend I didn't see *him*.' She waggled a finger at Jesse and looked stern. 'But I'm going to check on the system to make sure you get him thoroughly checked and properly registered, so make sure you do.'

Jesse started crying all over again at the woman's kindness. There was no ice left to cloak herself with; she was a mess.

*Two Months Later...*

Jesse took a deep breath and looked at herself in the floor-length mirror in her bedroom. The dress was a deep blue colour, and silk. It was a feat of designing that Jesse didn't understand. All she knew was that it showed far more skin than she was comfortable with. Practically her whole back was bare, apart from one strip of material connecting the front to the back, and it was very low-cut at the front.

Her fingers itched to take it off and put on a familiar dress suit, but then she remembered the spurt of something very illicit when she'd spotted it in the window of the shop in town that afternoon. She'd been trying it on before she'd even registered her intent, and the shop assistant had said, *'The dress was made for you. You have the perfect figure to carry it off...'*

Jesse knew it was just sales patter, but for a brief moment she'd felt something close to how she'd felt when Luc had looked at her naked body: beautiful and sensual.

*Luc.* Jesse shut the closet door on her reflection with force and hunted for the shoes she'd bought to go with the dress, resolutely pushing thoughts of him out of her mind with an effort. She was going to a charity auction tonight, in aid of a cause she supported. It was her first opportunity to *be* the kind of woman she'd always envied... And just like that her rebellious thoughts zeroed in on Luc again.

Ever since that Friday, which she'd dubbed Black Friday in her head, she'd been waiting for Luc to appear, thumping on her door or storming her offices. Demanding retribution. But the days and weeks had passed and he hadn't materialised.

Jesse had battled with a maelstrom of emotions when it had become clear that Luc had clearly washed his hands of her. If she'd needed confirmation of how little he would have cared for her under normal circumstances this was it. He didn't even care enough to punish her for thwarting his own plans for revenge.

Adding to the mix of emotions was the evidence she'd sought that had confirmed Luc's story was real. Every word. His father had been the poor but proud Spanish foreman at one of her father's construction sites and his wife a quiet

Frenchwoman. And his sister did indeed have special needs. Jesse had unearthed some pictures of him attending charity functions in aid of research into autism.

As for her father—he was well and truly finished. He was in hock to too many people, and a trial looked increasingly likely as all his various tax and fraud transgressions came to light. Not to mention mounting lawsuits from various employees who'd been intimidated into silence before, and were now coming forward with stories of harrassment, unfair dismissal and worse.

Even his wife was selling her story to the papers, depicting a tale of violent abuse for years. All his assets had been seized, and he was being watched to make sure he didn't flee the country.

Jesse had expected at least a feeling of euphoric triumph to know she'd finally seen to her father's end, but since it had happened she'd felt curiously empty and flat. On some level she did finally feel a sense of peace as if all that anger and rage and hurt had dissipated at last and been rendered impotent, but with shameful predictability her mind kept deviating not to her father or to the new lease of life she now faced, but to someone else...

The night after Luc had returned from the island he'd been splashed all over the news, appearing at a royal gala auction in aid of numerous charities with a stunning and recently Oscar-nominated actress on his arm. Since then he seemed to have been wining and dining a steady stream of women, each more beautiful than the last.

The press were in a frenzy. Luc Sanchis had never gone so overtly public before, and they couldn't get enough of it.

For a second Jesse stopped and closed her eyes, putting a hand to her chest as pain gripped her—she *had* to stop thinking about him. But it was impossible. She saw him everywhere, but paler imitations of him: today in the shop she'd nearly had a heart attack when a tall, dark, broad man had come in with his lover, a hand low on her back in a sexy caress. But it hadn't been him.

At night it was worse, when in dreams she relived in lurid detail every moment of those days on the island. She'd told him *everything*. Nothing had been sacred when she'd been indulging in a fantasy world and had forgotten why they were there in the first place.

Just then she felt a tugging sensation on the end of her dress and looked down to see Tigger about to sink a claw into the material. Jesse caught him up in her hands.

'Oh, no, you don't...'

She snuggled her face into his fur, relishing his warmth. He'd already grown and put on weight. She'd taken him to the vet and he'd been microchipped, vaccinated and even issued with his own passport. He was now a fully registered pet.

Jesse did feel pangs of guilt that she'd taken him from Luc, but she'd been in such turmoil that night as she'd got ready to leave that she hadn't been able to ignore the visceral impulse to take him with her. She needed him.

When he scrambled to be free again Jesse followed him out of her bedroom to the main living area. She took in the couch and table that had been delivered that week. And the TV.

Emotion made her chest tight. Finally she was beginning to move on with her life. She had a level of closure. What she'd always wanted. But, as much as she'd have liked to ascribe this long-overdue metamorphosis to seeing her father brought to justice, Jesse had to face the very uncomfortable suspicion that it had a lot more to do with Luc Sanchis and the change he'd precipitated within her on the island.

She heard the intercom announcing that her taxi had arrived and turned away from her thoughts with relief. She tried to ignore the giant-sized ache of loneliness in her chest. She

also tried to ignore the fluttering of anticipation in her belly
that just possibly Luc might have been invited to the event…

Luc looked out over the crowd in the thronged room. Men
were in tuxedos and women were in long glittering dresses.
He wanted to claw his own eyes out rather than be here at this
charity auction, but he'd promised his sister he'd bring her
and she was here somewhere now, with his mother, ogling as
many A-list celebrities as they could.

*Jesse.* Her name was like a ghostly whisper across his skin
and everything within Luc tensed. He could have laughed.
He'd been tense since he'd left that island. Since the night
*she'd* left the island. Since the night she'd taken his confi-
dences and trust and ground them beneath her feet.

He was angry. It was like a cold, hard piece of granite in
the centre of his chest that had the potential to explode at
any moment.

Once he'd known that O'Brien was well and truly finished—news he'd been furnished with on his recently returned phone somewhere over the Mediterranean Sea on that
private plane two months ago—Luc had felt something within
him shutting down and closing off.

Closing off the memory of standing in front of Jesse and
spilling his guts about his sad life story. Closing off the memory of losing sight of *why* he'd wanted to seduce her, because
once he'd tasted the nirvana of her body the last thing on his
mind had been getting off that island.

He thought of how he'd assured himself that he knew what
he was doing. But all along he'd been deluding himself…
weakened by the taste and touch of a woman. Letting her seduce him, *fool* him.

So he'd closed off those ten days on the island as effectively as if they had never happened.

Luc had returned to Britain and become an icy automaton.

Any rogue thoughts of Jesse were ruthlessly crushed at the merest whisper. His frenzy of socialising over the past couple of months had morphed into a blur of faces and places. But nothing had touched him. Nothing and no one had pierced through his shell.

His libido had spectacularly flatlined. But he didn't care, because the icy cold inside him was keeping his anger from exploding into a terrible fearsome thing.

*Jesse.* That ghostly sensation again, prickling across his skin. Luc cursed. It was as if that ice enclosing him was starting to melt away.

And then his eyes snagged on a head in the crowd. Short strawberry-blonde hair. Bare shoulders. A *dress*.

*Jesse.* She was no ghost. She was here, feet away. In a dress he'd never seen and holding a glass of champagne. The fact that she was alone and looking as vulnerable as she had the first time he'd seen her in a very similar milieu didn't penetrate.

All he could see was the pale expanse of bare back and a hint of the swell of her breast at the side of her ridiculously revealing dress. The way the silk clung to those lithe curves.

And suddenly his anger woke from its icy slumber and started to explode. And Luc knew in that moment what he wanted and what he needed.

*Revenge.*

As if Jesse had heard him thinking, felt the intensity of his gaze on her, she turned and saw him. Her eyes widened and the grey depths immediately darkened. Luc's libido surged back to life.

Revenge. And it would be sweet.

*Luc.* Here in this room. Her flutters of anticipation became tremors of reaction. The entire crowd became a blur of faceless people and the chatter a dim hum. All Jesse could see was that arresting rugged face. Unsmiling and more stark than she'd ever seen it. The lines of his body looked leaner, harder. His shoulders looked broader.

She felt weak all over. And emotion was bubbling upwards like a joyful fountain she couldn't control.

He came towards her and Jesse was rooted to the spot. When Luc was close enough for her to reach out and touch Jesse had to clench her hand into a fist by her side. The other hand was in a white-knuckle grip around a glass of champagne.

The air seemed to quiver with electric energy between them—but just then a young woman came up to Luc, taking his arm. The spell was broken and Jesse blinked. The woman was very pretty, with a long fall of glossy brown hair, dressed in a floor-length dress that was a little more demure than those worn by the other women around them.

She looked at Jesse in a way that wasn't polite, but wasn't exactly rude either. It was so open and guileless, almost child-like. And Jesse hadn't failed to notice how Luc's hand had come up to the woman's arm, as if to protect her. Jesse felt a crazy dart of hurt.

'Your hair is too short.'

Jesse looked at the woman. For a second her blunt words didn't sink in, and then Luc said stiffly, 'Eva, this is…someone I know. Jesse Moriarty.' He speared Jesse with a dark look. 'This is my sister—Eva Sanchis.'

*Someone I know.* The hurt spread outwards a little and Jesse avoided Luc's eyes. She could see the family resemblance now, and put out a hand to Eva. 'It's nice to meet you.' Her voice was husky with emotion.

Eva smiled and shook Jesse's hand. 'It's nice to meet you too. I'm sorry…about your hair.'

Jesse couldn't help a wry smile at her bluntness, not sure if she was apologising for what she'd said or because Jesse had such short hair. When Eva let go of her hand Jesse touched her hair lightly, and this time she really avoided Luc's eyes, because she could already feel a blush rising. 'I'm going to let it grow... I agree that it's too short. *You* have gorgeous hair.'

The woman grinned and looked up at her brother. 'She likes my hair.'

He smiled down at her indulgently, but Jesse could see his jaw was tight with tension. 'You do have beautiful hair, Eva. In fact I think you have the most beautiful hair in the room.'

His sister was practically bursting with pride, and Jesse felt acutely vulnerable. Naked. Which wasn't helped by the flimsy dress. She cursed herself for the weak impulse now... hating that she'd wanted to explore this hitherto hidden side of her nature...hating that Luc was here to witness it in such a fledgling and delicate stage.

She thought of the myriad women he'd been photographed with in the previous two months and stiffened her spine. Glancing at him without really looking at him, and encompassing his sister in her glance, she said, 'It was lovely to meet you, but if you'll excuse me there's someone I need to catch before they leave...'

Jesse stepped back, and as luck would have it someone cut in front of her at that moment. Without waiting for Luc or his sister to respond she turned and fled.

Luc swore under his breath when he saw Jesse dart away with a quicksilver flash of her blue dress. He heard Eva gasp at his side at his language, and forced his eyes off Jesse's progress to look down at his sister. Familiar feelings of love and protection swelled in his chest, and he welcomed them as an antidote to the extreme intensity of the much darker emotion he'd just been feeling.

His sister said, 'She was nice. I liked her. She's pretty, but she needs to grow her hair.'

Luc found himself smiling at his sister's remarkably simplistic take on meeting Jesse, and wished for a second it could be that easy. He reflexively searched for Jesse again but couldn't see her, and something within him solidified.

He wasn't finished with her. Not by a long shot.

# CHAPTER TEN

WHEN Jesse got back to her apartment she kicked off the high heels and paced her wooden floor, the silk dress swirling around her feet. She'd been terrified she wouldn't get out of that function and away from Luc. She was not even sure why she'd been so terrified, but there had been something so *unforgiving* about his expression.

Now she felt all jittery, and ridiculously energised. Tigger was curled up on the couch, and had just raised a sleepy head for a second before miaowing softly and going back to sleep.

Jesse hugged her arms around her body. The fact was when she'd seen Luc she'd had to battle an almost overwhelming urge to run straight into his arms. It was as if she'd blocked it out as soon as she'd felt it, but now it was crystalline in its intensity. Along with an aching yearning for him to have pulled her into his arms and hugged her close.

When he'd looked at his sister with such obvious affection jealousy had risen inside her like bile, almost choking her, but she'd kept it down with that superficial social nicety that had cloaked everything bubbling under the surface.

Jesse went and put her forehead against the glass of the huge window. London was spread out before her.

Seeing Luc again tonight had made her realise the cataclysmic revelation she'd been denying to herself ever since she'd left the island.

She was in love with him. Completely and irrevocably in love with him. No wonder she'd run...

A harsh knock sounded on her door and Jesse jumped and turned around, her heart almost pumping out of her chest. She could see Tigger standing on the couch, looking at the door too, as if he sensed something. *Or someone.*

Jesse walked over to the door and asked hesitantly, 'Who is it?'

'You know damn well who it is. Open up.'

Jesse sprang back and bit her lip, and then said, 'I don't think that's a good idea, Luc.'

His voice came back, low and guttural through the wood. 'I don't think it'll be a good idea to break this door down, but I fully intend to unless you open it right now.'

Little shards of sensation were racing up and down Jesse's body. Her skin felt hot, tight. What was he doing here?

With the utmost reluctance, and yet a treacherous excitement, Jesse walked forward and slid back the bolt before turning the latch and opening the door.

Luc was standing there, arms outstretched, hands resting on either side of the door. His bowtie was undone, top buttons open, jacket hanging loose. He looked dangerous and blisteringly angry. And sexier than she'd ever seen him.

'Damn you to hell, Jesse Moriarty. I hoped I'd never set eyes on you again.'

Jesse hitched up her chin, hoping he wouldn't see the hurt she felt on her face. But before she could say anything he'd closed the space between them, kicked the door shut and she was in his arms and his mouth was on hers, grinding soft skin into teeth. Suddenly Jesse didn't care. He was here, and his intensity told her that what had happened on the island, at least physically, *had* been real. That knowledge was heady.

She wound her arms around his neck and clung on for dear

life. Their mouths fused together, not even kissing properly, just touching as if starved of contact.

She could feel his hand on the back of her head, and her lungs were screaming for air, but she said nothing.

Suddenly Luc broke away. Jesse realised she was off her feet, lifted against his body. 'Damn you,' he said again throatily. And then, 'Where is your bedroom?'

Jesse couldn't seem to focus on anything rational. All she could feel were Luc's arms around her and his chest crushing her breasts. She wanted this. She needed this. She loved him.

'Behind me...'

Luc walked them into the bedroom. Jesse shivered at the tension in his body. Her nerves were tingling, her blood sizzling in her veins. When they got to her room Luc put her down and started to take off his jacket and bowtie to undo the buttons on his shirt, ripping it off.

Jesse was mesmerised by his chest, amazed at his sheer beauty—again.

'Take off your dress.'

It was a rough command. Jesse looked at Luc and tried to read his expression, but she couldn't. His eyes were so black. Something was amiss, but she couldn't put her finger on it and her brain was too overheated to work it out.

She reached behind her to where the ingenious fastening held the straps of the dress together. Immediately she could feel it give way, and brought her hands up to hold it in place.

'Let it go.'

Another rough command.

Jesse took her hands away and the dress fell to her waist. She could feel her breasts swell and tighten into sharp buds under Luc's gaze. She saw dark slashes of colour enter his cheeks.

He reached for his belt buckle and undid it, and then his trousers and pants were gone and he was naked. And aroused.

Suddenly he was kneeling at Jesse's feet, pushing up the silk skirt of her dress, pulling down her knickers at the same time, lifting her feet free of them one by one.

She felt his hands come to her thighs and push them apart. She staggered slightly, but kept her balance as Luc touched her intimately with his mouth.

Jesse gasped, her head thrown back, as Luc remorselessly relearned her most intimate parts. Her hands were on his head, fingers clutching at his hair. One of Luc's hands reached around and grabbed Jesse's buttock, squeezing its fleshy firmness.

Jesse was overwhelmed. Sensations were piling on top of sensations and her legs were like jelly. As if sensing how wobbly she was, Luc took his mouth from her and tipped her legs gently, so that she came down on the rug on the floor at the end of her bed.

As she watched Luc reached for the pocket of his trousers and took out something in a foil wrapper, ripping it with his teeth. She saw him take out protection and roll it onto his body. And then he came back and took her hands, held them together in one of his. He put them above her head and with his body spread her legs. The dress was bunched around her waist.

Jesse was so hot and aching inside that she rolled her hips and pleaded, 'Luc…'

'Yes,' he said gutturally. 'Say my name again.'

'Luc…'

And then he was there, pushing inside with ruthless intent, drawing a keening moan out of Jesse's mouth as her body accepted him and took him in greedily. He set up a rhythm that was designed purely to torture Jesse, she decided, as little beads of sweat broke out on her skin. She was shaking with the effort it took to hold on to whatever sliver of sanity she retained.

She felt wild and feral. Untamed. There was something so animalistic about this union. And then it broke over her—the sheer ecstasy she remembered. Except it was more, even more intense. With a shout Luc's movements became more frantic as the powerful pulsations of her body drove him over the edge too.

For a long moment Luc held himself suspended above Jesse, his hand still clasping hers, and then he let her go. Jesse lowered her arms and reached out to touch Luc's waist, but abruptly he pulled away from her, making her wince because her body was sensitive.

He stood up with a lithe movement and Jesse watched as he went into the bathroom. She felt exposed, lying on the rug with her dress bunched around her waist, and she had a prickling sensation of foreboding. Pushing her dress down and pulling it up over her breasts, she got up and sat on the end of her bed. She felt dizzy.

Just then Luc emerged from the bathroom, gloriously naked and utterly self-confident. Without looking at her he started to pull on his clothes.

The foreboding was growing. Jesse asked hesitantly, 'Where are you going?'

*Where are you going?*

Jesse's voice was soft, but it felt like rough sandpaper on Luc's skin. He called himself every name under the sun. He'd lost it completely as soon as Jesse had opened the door and he'd seen her standing there. All of his good intentions to be cool and icily controlled had fled, and been replaced by heat and lust. He'd had to have her. And so he'd taken her on the floor of her bedroom like some rutting animal. Once again proving her power over him, turning him into a base creature.

'Luc...?'

He gritted his jaw and finished buttoning up his shirt. He picked up his bowtie and jacket and turned to face her.

'Yes?' His voice was harsh.

He saw her expression falter…and even now he wanted her, with her kiss-swollen lips and flushed cheeks, her tousled hair…which was getting longer and making her look softer, even sexier. He thought of his sister and how Jesse had been so easy with her, not recoiling the way most people did when they realised that she wasn't quite…what they'd expected.

'What do you want, Jesse?' His voice was even more curt now. He wouldn't allow any weakness to invade him again. He welcomed his resolve and the banked anger within him. He drew on it.

Jesse stood up, holding her dress. She felt ridiculously vulnerable. Luc was acting like a cold stranger. 'I just… You're going…' It wasn't a question.

'Yes,' he said. 'I didn't come for cosy catch-ups and chats, Jesse. I came for one thing.'

Jesse fought not to wince. 'Sex.'

He shrugged minutely. 'In a word…yes. But not quite just sex.'

Jesse struggled to retain her dignity, even though it felt as if it was crumbling all around her. 'What else?'

He came close and ran a finger around the line of Jesse's jaw, and then his eyes rose to meet hers. 'Revenge, Jesse. You didn't seriously think you'd get away with what you did, did you?'

'What are you talking about?' It was a struggle to get the words out. Jesse's chest felt tight.

Luc's jaw clenched and he dropped his hand, but he didn't move back. 'What I'm talking about is retribution. A rebalancing of the scales, if you will. You single-handedly disrupted the course of my life and ruined plans I'd been working on for years.'

'But you know why that was,' Jesse reminded him painfully.

'Yes…just as *you* know what my reasons were for wanting the same outcome. But you didn't seem to think them compelling enough to take me with you when you left like a thief in the night.'

Jesse looked away, guilt lancing her. 'I'm sorry for leaving you on the island like that…but I couldn't afford to trust you.'

Luc's hand forced her face back to him, and she shivered at how stern he looked.

'Trust?' he spat out, as if it were a dirty word. 'Trust never came into it. Trust would imply that there was a relationship of some sort.'

Jesse's heart squeezed painfully, as if a vice were closing around it. She could feel her own anger rising at Luc, for being so cold and remote. Cruel.

She jerked her chin out of his hold and jabbed a finger towards his chest. '*You* seduced me just so that you could manipulate me into letting you go. I had *no* idea what your motives were.'

Luc smiled, and it was utterly bereft of emotion. 'I may have seduced you, Jesse, but it didn't take much persuasion…'

If Jesse hadn't been afraid of her dress falling down she would have hit Luc. He stepped back and turned to walk out of the room. Jesse rushed after him, anger boiling over and mixing with hurt.

'It's true what they said about that poor woman you ruined, isn't it? You weren't happy just to see her destroyed professionally. You had to make sure she had a breakdown because she had the gall to get one over on you.'

Abruptly Luc stopped, and Jesse almost ran into his back.

He turned around and she stepped back. The fact that he was so emotionless was worse than if he'd been breathing fire.

Icily he said, 'You know absolutely *nothing* about that woman or what happened at that time.'

Jesse ignored the voices in her head urging her to be quiet. She tossed her head and goaded him. 'So tell me—what do you have planned for me, Luc? Some similar dastardly fate for daring to cross you?'

Luc came towards her, menacing, until Jesse felt her back hit the wall. He loomed over her, and then Jesse felt him grab her dress in one hand and pull it down. She gasped but much to her shame and horror it wasn't fear she felt but a wild excitement. She tried to grab the dress back, but Luc was remorseless. He easily swatted her hands away and cupped her breast, his thumb lazily teasing the peak to embarrassing stiffness. Jesse fought back a moan and willed the heat in her body down.

'What I have planned for you, Jesse, is to be my very public companion, mistress, lover—whatever you want to call it—until such time as this annoying lust between us is burnt out and I'm satisfied. I'm going to take great pleasure in disrupting your life as much as I can.'

Jesse managed to pull Luc's hand off her breast and haul her dress back up. 'No. Tonight was a mistake and it won't be happening again. I can't believe that I was duped into thinking you were something different. That you were—'

Luc laughed out loud, throwing his head back for a moment. He looked down at her, 'What, Jesse? The besotted fool of the island?' He shook his head and smiled. 'So naive it's almost cute…'

Jesse managed to slither out from under his arm and stand apart from him. She was beginning to feel seriously undone, and she was afraid if he didn't leave right now she'd start crying or something equally pathetic.

She couldn't help blurting out, 'It's true, then? It *was* all an act—a grand seduction to try to force my hand.'

To her horror Luc merely started to look around her apartment, taking in the various furnishings and things.

Then he turned around and said coolly, 'What else could it possibly have been, Jesse? I had to use whatever means I could find, and I merely used the convenient chemistry between us. Any fool would have taken the same advantage.'

Feeling numb and hurt beyond belief at the man Luc had morphed into, she said, 'I should have left you there as soon as I'd got you into the villa.'

He came closer to her but she couldn't move. He touched her jaw with a finger and then smiled. 'Ah, but then you would have missed all that bedroom fun.'

Jesse jerked back as if he'd slapped her. And he might as well have.

'Get out, Sanchis. You've overstayed your welcome.'

She heard a miaow then, and saw Tigger at Luc's feet, front paws on one shoe. For a second the breath faltered in Jesse's throat. She saw Luc bend down and pick up the kitten, stroke him with those long fingers. It made her think of the frantic coupling that had just taken place with little or no finesse, just heat.

She hastily found the clasp at the back of her dress and did it up. She held out her arms for the kitten, demanding, 'Give him to me.'

Luc didn't look at her for a long moment, and Jesse had the awful suspicion that he might just walk out with him. But then Luc all but thrust Tigger into her arms.

He said, with a rough quality to his voice, 'I think he's hungry.'

And then he was at the door, where he stopped and looked back. 'I'll be in touch, Jesse.'

The door opened and he was gone.

For a moment, when he'd handed Tigger back to her, Jesse could have sworn she saw something piercing through the cold shell of the man he was now, but it had to have been her imagination.

Luc sat in the back of his car and stared sightlessly out of the window. He moved, and the scent of Jesse rose up to tease his nostrils. It had an immediate effect on his body, hardening it.

He scowled and ordered his driver to raise the privacy partition. He felt raw. When he'd seen the kitten at his feet, looking up at him just now, it had flung him back to the island, and the cool composure he'd somehow managed to pull around himself so that he could stand there and say those things to Jesse had threatened to crack.

But it hadn't, and he couldn't let it. The island had been an illusion. All along she'd been planning on leaving him there. When he thought of how confident he'd felt after he'd told her the truth about her father he felt the burning wash of humiliation. But not again. He wanted her, and he would take her. He wasn't going to go through with the pretence of seduction when there was no need. This time they both knew exactly where they stood.

Luc was aware that not even with Maria had he felt this ruthless, or *been* this ruthless. Despite the accusation Jesse had flung at him in her apartment. It reminded him of the the lurid tabloid headline: *Sanchis ex-lover tries to kill herself!* Accompanied by a story equally lurid, about how his ex-lover had betrayed him with a rival architect and he'd set out to get his revenge, driving her to the brink.

The truth was that it had been pure professional espionage. Maria had been the business partner and lover of a man whose company was a rival bidder for a lucrative architect contract. She'd set out to seduce Luc for her lover, purely to get his ideas and pass them on—which she had… And then Luc had lost the contract and a million euros' worth of investment.

It had almost been a killer blow, coming at a crucial stage in his career, just when he'd been on the cusp of achieving real respect. It had meant more long years of gruelling graft, building himself up again, building trust. The stain of infamy had lingered.

When Maria had returned to her lover to find him in the arms of another woman she'd gone on the attack and sold stories of her breakdown to the press—each one more lurid than the next—in a bid to make her lover take her back. She'd even staged a suicide attempt…and everyone had assumed Luc was the cause.

He shook his head now, as if to shake free of the memory. He didn't like to be reminded that he'd found it relatively easy to walk away from Maria after her betrayal, even though he'd never forgotten it. But with Jesse… He saw her and he wanted to possess her with something bordering on the obsessional.

He would have her, and this time it would be entirely on his terms. When this all-encompassing lust burnt out he would walk away. And then he would be free of any ghostly memories and her image plaguing him in his dreams every night.

The following day Jesse was on a conference call with her colleagues in Silicon Valley in California. She was gritty-eyed with lack of sleep and trying to force her foggy brain to try to keep up with the fast-flowing conversation.

She became vaguely aware of a kerfuffle of some sort outside her glass-walled office, and craned her neck to try to see what it was. When she did she almost dropped the phone. Luc was striding towards her office holding a huge box with a big pink ribbon around it, and her assistant Georgia was running after him, clearly trying to stop him from barging into Jesse's office.

Jesse almost felt sorry for Georgia, who had a look of awe mixed with lust mixed with fear on her face.

And then there he was, standing in her office, grinning at her. But Jesse could see the ice in his eyes. So nothing had changed there.

She said into the phone, 'I'm sorry, gentlemen, something has come up. I'm going to have to reschedule this call.'

She put down the phone and got up and went to the door.

Georgia was outside, blushing. 'I'm really sorry, Jesse, he just—'

Jesse stopped her. 'It's fine. I'll handle it.'

She closed the door and turned to face Luc, who was looking around her office with interest. Jesse wasn't unaware of lots of eyes checking them out, and cursed the fact that she'd insisted on glass-walled offices to foster a sense of openess.

She went back to her desk and sat down, trying to assert her authority—which was laughable. She had no authority around this man. He came over and put the box down on her desk. He leant over it and Jesse fought not to slink back into the chair, or let her eyes dwell on his hard-boned face.

'Considering how generous you were in giving me a wardrobe of clothes on Oxakis, I've decided to return the favour.'

Jesse glanced at the box suspiciously, as if it might explode, and then back at Luc. 'What is it?'

He stood back. 'Take it out and have a look.'

Colour flared into Jesse's cheeks and she glanced around her. She saw several heads quickly swivel back to work. She could well imagine Luc had chosen something to mete out as much humiliation as possible.

She hissed at him, 'You can't just come in here like this. I'm busy. That was an important call you interrupted.'

Luc quirked a brow. 'You mean like the way you *didn't* barge into my office and demand to be heard?'

Jesse flushed even more. So he was following through on his promise of retribution.

She reached for the box and ripped off the bow. 'If it's the only way to get rid of you...'

The top of the box came off to reveal gold tissue paper. Jesse pushed it aside to see champagne-coloured folds of material peeping out. Intrigued despite herself, Jesse lifted out the dress. It was strapless and short—exactly the kind of dress she'd seen other women wearing and envied.

She avoided Luc's eye, feeling horribly vulnerable. 'I don't wear things like this. It won't suit me.'

'Well, I have a yen to see you in a short dress, so you're wearing it tonight, at the opening of a gallery in town.'

Before she could respond to his autocratic statement he came and sat on the side of her desk, for all the world as if this was a daily occurrence.

'Keep going. There's more,' he said.

For a second Jesse's heart clenched hard, painfully. What if things had been different...? What if what had happened on the island between them had been real...?

Mortified to find her thoughts straying into such dangerous territory, she scrabbled through the rest of the tissue and pulled something out. She only realised that she was holding up a strapless wisp of lace that was masquerading as a bra very belatedly, and with cheeks burning stuffed it back into the box.

She stood up, and was not prepared when Luc reached over, put his hand around the back of her neck and pulled her close before slanting his mouth over hers.

But this wasn't like last night's desperate kiss. This was slow and searching, almost tender, and Jesse had to cling on to the desk when her legs grew wobbly. Luc's tongue teased her lips, and on a helpless sigh she opened them.

And then, just as suddenly, Luc had pulled away and was

standing up, leaving Jesse still comically leaning forward. She sprang back and her eyes spat sparks at him.

He chuckled darkly. 'Don't look so fierce. I'm doing your reputation a favour, you know. They say you're quite the cold fish, but we know otherwise—don't we, Jesse?'

Before she could explode he'd blown her a kiss and was striding back out of her office. Jesse couldn't be unaware of the sudden flurry of whispers, or the way several female and some male heads swivelled in his direction for a long time. She sat down and angrily stuffed the dress into the box, then put it on the floor beside her.

She felt that dreaded emotion rising again, and willed it down with everything in her body. She desperately longed to tell Luc where he could shove his non-invitation to go out that evening, but was all too aware that he would most likely steamroller his way over her refusal and come to her apartment and dress her himself...and that thought had a burst of heat flooding her lower body.

Jesse had to face the fact that she'd created this monster by kidnapping him in the first place. All she could do for now was go along with him. She had no doubt that with a willing line of beauties waiting for him in the wings whatever appeal Jesse held for him would soon wane. And then she would deal with the fall-out—far away from Luc's prying mocking gaze.

That evening Luc knocked on Jesse's door impatiently. Something uncomfortably like panic gripped him inside when there was no immediate answer. If she was going to try to—

The door opened suddenly to reveal Jesse standing there, looking hassled in a robe, holding Tigger. She thrust the kitten at Luc and said, 'He wrecked the kitchen while I was out today. I've just spent an hour cleaning it up. I'll be ready in ten minutes.'

And she disappeared.

Luc stepped into the apartment holding Tigger, who was looking entirely innocent of any crimes, purring contentedly into Luc's palm.

This scenario was so far removed from Luc's normal experience with women that it took a minute to orientate himself. He was used to being greeted by women dressed to impress: coiffured and perfumed and *haute coutured* to within an inch of their lives.

He went and sat down in the one armchair, and Tigger curled trustingly into his lap. Luc realised that he'd missed the tiny animal. He'd been even angrier with Jesse when he'd discovered she'd not only left the island but taken the kitten too. It had been like a double betrayal.

He took in the spartan nature of her apartment. It looked as if she'd only just moved in, but Luc knew she'd had it for a few years. The ascetic nature of the space matched her style the day she'd come to see him in his office.

She'd been zealous and single-minded that day. Sitting here now, he could all too easily imagine her returning after that meeting, having nothing on her mind but how to make sure her father was ruined, and how she could stop Luc from getting in her way...

Thinking of her like that...on her own, fighting...made something weaken in Luc's chest. And then he heard a sound and looked up. And couldn't breathe for a long second.

Jesse stood on the far side of the room, obviously nervous. But all he could see were her legs, looking stupendously long and shapely in the pair of gold sandal heels that had come with the dress. The dress reached to midthigh and fell from a ruched bodice in soft folds to her knees. The bodice hugged her breasts, making them seem fuller.

Her skin glowed like a lustrous pearl next to the champagne colour, and Luc's body tightened painfully when he thought of the freckles on her skin that were only visible up close. He carefully put Tigger down and stood up, oblivious to the kitten's indignant miaow. Luc felt very uncharacteristically at a loss.

Jesse felt like a child trying to play at dress-up who'd ended up looking like a clown. She'd put on make-up but, not used to it, had probably put on too much. Luc was just staring at her, as if she were some kind of alien.

She turned to go back into her room and change, saying, 'I told you it wouldn't suit me. These kind of clothes just don't—'

She was whirled around and she gasped. She hadn't even heard Luc move. His hands were around her face and the look in his eyes was *hot*. It reminded her of how he'd looked at her before.

'It's beautiful—perfect. You look stunning in it. I like what you did with your hair...'

Jesse blushed and put a hand up, embarrassed. She was so happy to see it growing out a bit that she'd experimented by putting a small plait into her fringe to keep it out of her eyes. She'd completely forgotten to take it out. 'That was just messing. I can't go out like this...'

Luc stilled her hand with his and said, 'It's cute. Leave it.'

Jesse grimaced and glanced up at him, far too aware of how potent he was in dark trousers and a light shirt, open at the neck. 'It's silly.'

He shook his head. 'It's sexy.'

Jesse found it hard to breathe, and then she heard a miaow at her feet and looked down to see Tigger, winding his way between their touching toes. The image was curiously intimate, and Jesse bent down to pick him up before Luc could see her expression. She took Tigger into the kitchen and put him in his box for the night, making sure he had food and milk.

When she went back out to Luc the moment seemed to have passed, and he was looking stern again.

He put out a hand. 'Come on or we'll be late.'

Jesse resisted the urge to do something childish, like stick out her tongue, and instead put her hand in his. There was something so intimate about the gesture in the midst of all the tension that she stumbled a little, cursing him for not making it easier to resist his charm.

Luc looked at her in the lift. His voice sounded tight as he remarked, 'You're not used to high heels, are you?'

Jesse shook her head, glad that he thought it was just the shoes keeping her off balance.

In the back of his car, as they wound their way through London at dusk, Jesse couldn't stop herself from saying, 'You've been busy since—' She stopped abruptly.

Luc supplied the missing words. 'Since my incarceration on that island?'

Jesse looked at him for an unguarded moment. Did he really see it as just that? She answered herself. Of course he did.

She tried to get out of it, sorry she'd opened her mouth. 'I just meant you seem to have been…going out…'

'With a lot of women?' he supplied helpfully.

Jesse flushed.

Luc reached across the divide and ran a finger down the line of one bare shoulder. Jesse could feel herself responding, melting.

'Jealous, Jesse?'

'Don't be ridiculous,' she snapped, and moved back so his hand dropped.

But she was. She was piercingly, achingly jealous. Jealous of any moment another woman got to spend alone with this man, talking just to him, having him look at her as if she was the only one there. Kissing her. The pain was so acute that Jesse curled right back into the corner and turned away from Luc. She shouldn't be jealous, because this wasn't the Luc she'd fallen for...

She forced out more forcibly, 'Don't be ridiculous.'

# CHAPTER ELEVEN

Luc looked at the tense line of Jesse's shoulders and fought the urge he had to snarl at his driver to raise the privacy division. He wanted to take her right there and then, sliding her onto his lap. Her dress was so short all he'd have to do was unzip his trousers.

Luc ripped his eyes off Jesse and beat back the waves of heat consuming him. Damn her for having this effect on him so easily. He might have imagined that in the civilised surroundings of a city he wouldn't want her so badly, but he wanted her even more…

A little later, when they were in the gallery, Luc looked around with irritation. *Where was she?* He'd never known a woman not to cling on to him like a limpet in social situations, but as soon as they'd arrived Jesse had shown a genuine interest in the paintings and moved off to look at them on her own. Luc did not like to analyse how that made him feel.

He went into the other room, where the auctioneer for the artists was shaking Jesse's hand effusively. She was putting what looked like a credit card back into her bag.

Luc came alongside her and she looked up and blushed. 'I just wanted to pay for the paintings.'

'You bought some?'

She nodded, her eyes gleaming for a moment. 'The big one of the reeds on the canal and a couple of smaller ones.'

Luc observed dryly, 'Your apartment does seem some-what bare...'

Jesse blanched a little and mumbled something like, 'I'm buying more stuff for it now.'

He caught her arm and made her look up at him. 'Why is it so bare, Jesse?'

For a long moment she just looked at him, and then she said huskily, 'Because for a long time I haven't cared about much else.'

Luc was sorry he'd asked, because his chest felt tight. He should have known not to expect a glib answer from Jesse. Wordlessly he ushered her back into the main gallery, but his mind was in a tumult and he felt something like panic rising up to strangle him.

When they got into Luc's car a short time later Jesse immediately took off her sandals with an appreciative groan. She didn't care at this stage what Luc's usual women might do. She was in agony. She was also feeling mildly merry after a couple of glasses of wine, and buoyed up from buying those paintings. She realised that she'd actually had a nice time this evening, despite the tense undercurrents. She turned to tell Luc, but closed her mouth abruptly. He was looking stonily out of his window, his profile harsh and forbidding.

Jesse wanted to reach over and touch his face, and before she knew she'd even moved she found herself kneeling on the seat next to him. He turned and looked at her and she reached out to cup his jaw, her heart beating fast. If he was cruel now, or said something... But he didn't. He put his hands on her hips and brought her round to straddle his lap, her legs either side of his powerful thighs, and all she could see was Luc... *her* Luc...with those dark, fathomless molten eyes.

Jesse could feel where his hardness pushed against their clothes and liquid heat surged between her legs. She put her hands around Luc's face and bent down to kiss him, feeling as if she were falling into a dark chasm.

He cupped her head, his other hand on her bottom, urging her even closer to him. The kiss rapidly got out of control, flames licking around them. Jesse found the buttons on his shirt and opened them, wanting to feel his skin. Luc was pulling down her dress so that one breast was bared...

She barely heard him give curt instructions to the driver, and then urgency overtook them. His mouth was on her breast, sucking her nipple deep, rolling his tongue around the hard tip. Jesse was desperate to feel him inside her and had reached down between them to find his belt buckle, almost sobbing with frustration when she couldn't get it open immediately.

Luc made fast work of freeing himself. Jesse wrapped her hand around him and stroked him, and Luc's face tightened with a need that looked feral in the dim light. He took her hand away and found her knickers, drawing them to the side before he stroked one finger along her cleft. Jesse moaned softly, dizzy with need.

And then Luc positioned her and brought her down on top of him, slowly and inexorably, until he was buried in her. With a rocking movement Jesse clenched and unclenched her muscles in a completely instinctive rhythm. They both climaxed within minutes.

It was silently intense. Jesse collapsed against Luc, and after a moment could feel his hand come to her back, holding her. She felt tears prick her eyes at the gesture, but was very afraid that he wouldn't relish her feeling so emotional right now.

After a minute Jesse was feeling increasingly exposed and vulnerable. She extricated herself from Luc's embrace and sat on the seat, pulling her dress down. She felt cheap. It was hard to believe the car was still moving.

'Where are we going?'

Luc's voice was sterile. 'I'm taking you home.'

She looked at him and he turned to face her. She nearly recoiled at the harshness of his expression. She'd thought him cold before, but she could barely fathom that this was the man who had just brought her over the edge in his arms. She had to remember that it had been she who'd climbed all over him, pathetically convincing herself she'd seen something in his eyes.

Mortified, she turned away. 'Thank you.'

To her surprise she felt Luc's hand on her jaw, turning her back to face him. She steeled herself.

For a long moment he said nothing, and Jesse recognised with a jolt that they were already pulling up outside her apartment. That had been the guttural instruction to his driver.

'Luc...?'

She had no prickling of foreboding, no idea of what was coming. And when the words were delivered, Luc's voice was so flat he might have been talking about stocks and shares.

'We're done, Jesse. Our little interlude is over.'

Luc's hand dropped from her jaw and he sat back. Jesse just stared at him. All she could think about was that he'd held her aloft again for a brief moment and was now letting her smash to the ground. *Revenge. Retribution.* Such ineffectual words for the feelings blooming inside her like blood spreading on the ground.

Pathetically, it had to be the quickest revenge in history— a mere couple of days and nights. A maelstrom was erupting in her chest—so many emotions that she didn't know which was uppermost. Hurt. Anger. Pain, yes. That was there more than all of them. Pain because she'd been so weak. She'd lain down and let him take her when all he'd wanted to do was punish her. It had only taken a quickie on her bedroom rug and another in his car for him to become bored.

Incensed, and galvanised by a force greater than she'd ever

felt, Jesse reached over and slapped Luc across the face. It was awkwardly delivered, but he didn't move or flinch. She wanted to hit him again so badly she shook with it.

'You bastard,' she said shakily. 'You absolute bastard.'

And then he said, 'Just go, Jesse. Get out.'

Jesse didn't need any encouragement. She scrambled out of the car and slammed the door, standing on the pavement and fighting down the tremors starting to rack her body with shock and pain. She wanted to watch him drive away, etch it onto her memory so she would never be so duped again.

The door opened. Luc was holding out her shoes.

Jesse spat at him, 'Keep them. You bought them anyway, and if you can find a mistress with the same shoe size you can use them again—impress her with your recessionary scruples.'

Luc just dropped them to the gutter and the door closed. The car pulled away. The back wheel drove over one of the shoes, crushing it. Jesse stood at the side of the road, barefoot, and her heart splintered into a million pieces, each one cutting her like glass.

As his car drove off, all Luc could feel was a dull ache. Not even the tingling of his cheek where Jesse had slapped him. He closed his eyes, but he could still see how she'd looked just now—as if he'd slapped *her*. Then all he could see was the intent expression on Jesse's face as she'd come over to touch his face, effortlessly sensing his black mood. And then the expression on her face as she'd slid onto him, taking him into her tight, silky embrace.

His eyes snapped open again. He'd set out to get revenge, but within just thirty-six hours things were already derailing fast. Again. It had happened on the island and now here. The woman seemed to have some innate ability to burrow under Luc's skin and lodge there like a thorn, sending him spinning in a million different directions at once.

On some level he'd been confident that Jesse would instantly morph into a woman he knew how to handle, but she hadn't. And she couldn't. Because she was utterly different. She was achingly sexy and vulnerable. Yet stronger than anyone he'd ever known. And the truth was she made him feel weak.

As he'd held her on his lap just now, in his arms, something soft had been cracking him open all over again, making him as vulnerable as he'd been on the island.

In the aftermath of that shattering climax Luc had seen only one possible outcome. She had to go. His very life depended on it—the life he knew, the life he'd built up around himself and his family with ruthless intent. Jesse threatened the equilibrium he'd worked so hard to achieve every time he looked at her, smelled her scent.

He should have just ignored her the other evening. That would have been revenge enough. But he'd been weak. He'd had to have her. He wouldn't be so weak again. It was over. His and Jesse's lives had entwined for a brief moment in time. That was all it was and all it ever would be.

He didn't want her in his life. It was that simple. He needed to feel in control, and control was in very short supply around Jesse Moriarty.

As Luc's car cut through the light night-time London traffic he relished the prospect of his life finally returning to normal and ignored the dull ache in his chest. A dull ache was nothing. He could cope with a dull ache over the almost painful intensity Jesse threatened him with...

*Two Weeks Later...*

Luc sat on the edge of the bed in his New York apartment's bedroom. Downtown Manhattan was laid out before him. Usually it inspired him with an incredible sense of energy. Except energy was in short supply, and had been for two weeks now. He felt nothing but numb—as if something had died inside him when he'd driven away from Jesse that night.

She was everywhere. In his thoughts, in his dreams. Only yesterday he'd stepped out of his offices and a woman had careened into him, small with short strawberry-blonde hair. Luc's heart had spasmed so violently he'd felt dizzy as he'd reached out to grab her shoulder. The woman had looked back. She wasn't Jesse. Nothing like Jesse, and she'd shouted an expletive to Luc, telling him to keep his hands to himself...

Biting back a groan, Luc stood up and noticed that he'd left the TV on all night on mute. He grimaced at this evidence of his sleeplessness, and was about to turn off the rolling English news channel when his hand stilled on the remote and his breath dried in his throat.

It was Jesse, and this time she wasn't a mirage. She was struggling through a mob crowd outside her apartment, with only a security guard to help her, and she looked tiny and defenceless.

Suddenly the numbness disappeared and feeling rushed back into Luc's body with such force he almost staggered. In that moment his heart cracked into two pieces and he knew he'd made the biggest mistake of his life.

Jesse was trying very hard not to let terror grip her into a state of paralysis.

The security guard on the phone sounded weary. 'They're still here, love. Looks like they're settling in for the night too.'

Jesse put down the phone and blinked back the onset of weak tears. If anything had shown her the depth of hatred and resentment Luc felt for her this had. She'd been under siege in her apartment for two days now—ever since someone had leaked to the press who she was. The disgraced JP O'Brien's daughter.

She found it easier to keep the incredible hurt and pain at bay if she focused on hating him.

Her phone rang and she picked it up, saying automatically, 'No, I'm not interested in giving a—'

'Jesse…it's me.'

For a second she was in shock, and then Luc's deep voice lanced her like a poison arrow. She laughed and it verged on hysteria. 'Tell me, did you come up with this plan as a little something to keep you occupied because you had no one else to torture?' She shouted down the phone. 'Just stay away from me, Sanchis!'

This time after she put the phone down she pulled the cord from the wall.

After a few minutes she heard an e-mail ping in on her home computer and went and sat down.

She opened it up and the first words she saw were: *Jesse, don't stop reading this, please.*

Tigger had somehow got onto the table. Almost absently Jesse scooped him onto her lap. Against her best intentions she read Luc's e-mail. He claimed not to be involved in leaking the story to the press and said that he'd only just seen the news in New York, that he would come over as soon as he got back to see if she was all right. He also went into a lengthy explanation of what had happened all those years ago with his ex-lover.

Jesse was dangerously close to unravelling at this e-mail. 'Why does he care what I think anyway?' she muttered to herself, looking at his e-mail again. He felt guilty. That had to be it. Guilty—and perhaps he pitied her too.

She got panicky when she imagined him arriving at her door, ordering her to open up with that deep voice, threatening to kick it down if she didn't. She couldn't forget the devastation she'd felt when he'd thrown her out of his car and his life. The devastation that still lacerated her insides.

She replied:

Don't write to me again. Don't come near my apartment. Leave me alone or I will call the police.

Two days later Jesse sent up silent thanks that she was due to go to Oslo for a few days of meetings about investing in one of their biggest gaming consortiums. She was escaping the intense press interest, that was the main thing, and also escaping the endless round of thoughts that seemed determined to circle on Luc Sanchis.

He hadn't appeared at her apartment, threatening to knock her door down, and Jesse hated herself for being so disappointed. She had told him not to come near her. She was worse than pathetic.

As she settled into the private jet that had been sent for her by the Norwegian company she relished the privacy. Some hair flopped forward onto her forehead and Jesse pushed it back, enjoying this proof that her life was changing in subtle ways all the time.

She was infinitely softer than she had been. Even her clothes were softer. She felt a little exposed in loose harem-style pants, with a slim gold belt and a soft clinging top, but she couldn't go back to the asexual uniform she'd worn before. And she hated that her metamorphosis had more to do with one person than her own desire to change: *Luc.*

Once they were cruising Jesse switched on her laptop. It opened straight onto Luc's e-mail. She couldn't help but touch the screen with her fingers, as if she could touch him. The last words of his message blinked out at her: *I've never felt the desire to set this story straight with anyone except you...*

Jesse resolutely deleted the e-mail and crushed all thoughts of Luc Sanchis. She was barely clinging on to control as it was.

It was only when she realised she hadn't seen the polite air steward who had helped her onto the plane for a while that she began to get a little suspicious. Also, she had the weird sensation that they weren't flying so much west to east across northern Europe as north to south.

She looked out of the window and the topography definitely looked browner than it should, given that they should almost be descending over Norway by now. In fact the plane didn't seem to have dipped in altitude at all yet.

Jesse began to panic mildly, but told herself that she was being ridiculous. But as the minutes ticked by and the plane droned onwards, flying further and further into territory that bore no resemblance to Norway, she panicked in earnest.

She got out of her seat and knocked on the main pilot's door, where the steward had to be too. No answer. Something was definitely up. Jesse sat back down, sweating now. She could see the sea below her and it sparkled in the sunlight. Azure blue and green. An awful suspicion was forming in her head, but she didn't dare give it oxygen so she sat rigidly in her seat and focused on staying calm.

By the time the plane did land, and a sheepish-looking air steward emerged from the cockpit, Jesse was feeling rage. This was the last straw. She all but sprang out of her seat and went to the open door of the plane. She looked out onto exactly the same peaceful idyllic scene Luc Sanchis had greeted months before—only this time the roles were reversed.

She looked down to see him standing at the side of the Jeep, hands in the pockets of his jeans, a short-sleeved polo shirt straining across his chest. Dark glasses glinted in the sun.

In the space of time since they'd been here the temperature had already risen, and it held the promise of the heat of summer not far away.

Jesse crossed her arms against the emotion in her chest and shouted out, 'I'm not getting off this plane, Sanchis!'

She watched as Luc ripped his sunglasses off and threw them into the Jeep beside him. He started striding towards her and Jesse squeaked and ran back into the plane, buckling herself back into her seat. The air steward looked on, impassive.

She heard Luc coming up the metal steps, and then he was filling the doorway with his broad frame.

'How many times do I have to tell you not to call me Sanchis? We're way beyond that now.'

Jesse felt breathless. 'I'm not leaving, Luc.' She appealed to the steward. 'This man is kidnapping me.'

'Well, in fairness, Ms Moriarty, I think you kidnapped him first.'

Jesse blanched and far too belatedly recognised the young man as the steward she'd hired herself to slip the sleeping aid into Luc's drink that day. This was how scrambled her brain had become. Her heart sank.

Luc looked smug, and then he was advancing on her, bending down, effortlessly flipping open the safety belt. Jesse was trying to swat his hands away but to no avail. Before she knew it Luc was hefting her over his shoulder in a fireman's lift.

She was speechless and slightly winded. She was vaguely aware of the steward carrying some things out of the plane—*her* things—and going ahead of them, presumably to put them in the Jeep. As he went past them again, back towards the plane, she heard Luc say, 'Thanks, Steven. I'll call your boss when I want you to come back. It might be a few days.'

Jesse gasped and hit Luc's back. 'Stop this! Put me down!' But her words were weak and ineffectual from this position.

She heard the steps being pushed away and the plane's engine revving up and clenched her hands into fists. Luc got to the Jeep and put her down, all but lifting her into the passenger seat, securing the seat belt around her before closing her door.

He was in the driver's seat and locking the doors from the inside before she'd even got her breath back. She was sputtering and gasping with indignation, and then Luc looked at her and grinned.

'I have to admit this is far more satisfying than I expected it to be.'

He turned back and, much more expertly than Jesse had, drove them off the airfield and to the villa. Jesse sat and fumed, arms crossed. And secretly battled the million butterflies that were hopping around in her belly. She kept her eyes forward, averting them from Luc's big, capable hands and his thighs in those faded jeans.

Jesse heard a sound from the back of the Jeep. She looked back and gasped when she saw Tigger was in a cat basket. She glanced at Luc. 'But…how?'

Jesse had only that morning left him with her apartment security guard, who'd assured her that his daughter would take care of Tigger.

Luc didn't answer straight away. He drove through the gates of the villa, pressing the button to close them behind him, but Jesse was barely aware of that. All sorts of emotions were erupting in her belly. Why had he brought Tigger? What did it mean?

Luc cast her a quick glance. 'Deborah, my secretary, explained the situation to your security guard. She brought Tigger to the plane just ahead of your arrival.'

Jesse sat back in the seat. They were pulling up to the villa now, and she said suspiciously, 'What situation?'

Luc stopped the Jeep smoothly, undid his belt and got out. He then took out Tigger's basket and came around to open Jesse's door. She scrambled out before he could touch her, far too aware of how it had felt to be thrown over his shoulder.

She asked again. 'What situation?'

Luc just strode ahead of her and said, 'Patience is a virtue, Jesse.'

Jesse slammed the Jeep door shut, feeling like a petulant child. With no choice, she followed him into the hallway. She said to his back, 'What about my meetings? I'm expected in Oslo right now.'

Luc turned around. 'I took the liberty of tracking down one of the few hackers out there *not* employed by you and paid him to hack into your account. I got him to send e-mails postponing all your meetings. You might want to look into hiring him as he did such a good job.' He gestured with a hand. 'I don't think I need to show you around, do you? Your tour was quite comprehensive the last time.'

He turned again and started striding towards the kitchen. Jesse followed him with hands clenched, still in shock that he'd turned the tables so neatly on her.

'Luc…'

When she got there he'd put Tigger's basket down and let him out, and the fast-growing kitten was already frolicking in the grass and running after butterflies.

'Luc—'

He went to the cooker and she could see that something was already on the stove, cooking. He'd obviously been here for a while and had started preparing food.

He glanced up, for all the world as if this was an entirely normal occurrence. 'I made some pasta for lunch. You're probably hungry, and I know how crabby you get if you don't eat properly.'

Jesse just blinked at him. Something much more volatile was happening inside her now. Emotion was cracking and spreading. 'Luc, what are you *doing*?'

He ignored her and came to steer her into a chair; he poured ier some wine. 'Just...relax, Jesse. We'll eat and then talk, okay?'

Jesse watched him as he went back to tend to the food. She might almost have imagined that he sounded *nervous*, and those emotions in her belly grew a lot more tangled and volatile.

For once Jesse was happy not to push it, afraid of what he might say, and a couple of minutes later Luc served her up a delicious-looking plate of *penne* in a simple tomato sauce, with crusty bread.

They ate, and it was the most surreal meal Jesse had ever had, with neither of them saying a word.

When they were finished Jesse cleared the plates. A strong feeling of *déjà-vu* caught her unawares, making her stumble slightly. Past and present were dangerously meshed. She had to grip the sink for a moment.

Luc was beside her instantly, arms around her. 'What is it?'

Jesse felt herself responding helplessly and emotion surged dangerously. She pushed herself free, terrified Luc would see how much it was affecting her to be back here.

She backed away from him, eyes huge. 'Is this some kind of elaborate sick joke, Luc? The last laugh is on you because you've managed to kidnap me?'

He shook his head. His eyes were intense. 'No, it's not a joke, Jesse. I've never been more serious about anything in my life.'

Suddenly Jesse blurted out, '*Stop* it—stop making me think that—' She couldn't finish. She turned and fled the kitchen, needing to hide her raw emotions from Luc.

But he followed her to the den, to the couch where he'd first made love to her. It sat between them, reminding her, making that emotion crack open even more.

'Making you think what, Jesse?'

She swallowed, desperately clinging on to whatever flimsy

control she had left. 'What are we doing here, Luc? Why did
you do this? More punishment? You weren't satisfied that I'd
quite got the message?'

He winced, and his face took on a slightly ashen hue.
'Jesse, if I could go back in time to when we met again, to
that last night in particular, and change what I did and said
I would. I was unforgivably cruel and a coward.'

Jesse put her hand to her belly, feeling sick to remember
it. 'You didn't have to bring me all this way just because you
feel bad about how you ended it, Luc, or bad about what happened. I knew it was never going to be anything more.'

He smiled then, but it was bleak. 'Did you, Jesse? Then
you knew more than me—even though I told myself I knew
what I wanted, knew what I was doing.'

Jesse was getting confused. Luc looked almost sad now.

'I brought you here, Jesse, because this is where it ends...
if it has to end.'

Jesse's heart spasmed. 'I thought it *had* ended.'

To her surprise Luc said, 'That night when we first met
over a year ago. You were there because your father was
there, weren't you?'

Jesse nodded. 'It was the first time I'd seen him since I
was a child. I'd gone there because I needed to know what
was up against.'

Luc ran a hand through his hair, tousling it. His eyes
speared her to the spot. 'It started between us that night,
Jesse, and then afterwards when you came to my office. It's
so ironic that we wanted the same thing, yet both of us were
so used to trusting only ourselves we didn't even think to
consider that option.'

Jesse grimaced. 'The evidence pointed towards us each believing the other wanted to go into business with my father...
I couldn't afford to let you know my motives because I didn't
want anyone to know about my relationship with him.' She

bit her lip. 'It felt like such an ugly part of me... How could I articulate that? Or why I wanted to destroy him?'

Luc was shaking his head. 'After you left here...left me here...I spent those two days devising every torture possible to inflict upon you when I saw you again. And then when I learned that O'Brien was really gone, that you'd got him, I realised that I wasn't even angry about that—after years of wanting to avenge my father. O'Brien had stopped being a priority for me around the same time as I got off that plane and realised you'd kidnapped me. That's how quickly you made me forget nearly everything. I was angry about something else entirely. Angry at how easily you'd managed to make me forget everything I'd believed was important. Angry at how hurt I was that you couldn't trust me.'

Luc continued before Jesse could interject.

'So to cope with that knowledge I simply blocked you out completely. I shut down. If I could have had an operation to erase you from my memory bank I would have, because I knew how dangerous you were to me by then. I dated a different woman every night in some kind of effort to feel normal again, and within five minutes of meeting each woman I wanted to claw my own eyes out from sheer boredom.'

Shakily Jesse said, 'That's a pretty strong reaction.'

'Yes.' Luc was grim. 'Because pretending you hadn't ever existed was slowly driving me insane—and then I saw you, at that function... To try to avoid how I was really feeling about seeing you again, I told myself I wanted revenge for what you had done. But really I wanted revenge for how you made me feel. For making me relegate everything that had been important in my life to the periphery—like my mother and sister. You waltzed into my office like a tiny tornado, wreaking havoc, and I should have known then that I was in trouble.'

Jesse needed to sit down. Her legs felt wobbly. She looked behind her and saw a chair and sank into it. Luc came closer and she was glad she was sitting down. He pulled the matching chair close and sat down too. Jesse found it hard to breathe.

She needed to speak, to say something. 'You said that there was no trust between us because there was no relationship.'

Luc just looked at her, searching her face as if for a clue. And then he said heavily, 'I wanted to hurt you in return for not trusting me, so I said that. But it was cruel and untrue...'

Jesse forced herself to be strong, not to let her heart take flight to a place that might not even exist, no matter how mesmerising Luc's eyes were. 'I know you just seduced me to try to manipulate me, though. You can't deny that.'

Luc shook his head. 'No, I can't deny it. But I soon forgot why I'd wanted or needed to seduce you in the first place. That's why it hurt so much when you left that night. It hadn't even occurred to me that you might not trust me...'

Feeling threatened and exposed, Jesse sprang up and started to pace. Luc was too close, too distracting.

She turned around. 'That day...the day you realised the truth about my father...I felt like I was coming to my senses. It terrified me how much I'd lost track of everything and to realise how close I'd come to trusting you completely when you still had the power to save my father. I was afraid you were making everything up.'

Jesse's hands clenched together.

'I told myself I couldn't believe in anything that had happened. I'd forced us into this situation. You told me yourself you'd do anything to get off the island. And then when you told me about *your* father...'

Jesse felt emotion rising inexorably and looked at Luc. He stood up, and she faced him squarely and leaped into the terrifying darkness.

'The truth is that I wanted to believe in you so badly, and I wanted to believe in what had happened here, between us... wanted to believe it was more than just manipulation or seduction…and that scared me to death. I didn't want to go back to reality with you and find out that once you were free you'd walk away…'

'I wouldn't have walked away, Jesse, and realising that only made me want to punish you more,' Luc said softly.

She put a hand to her mouth to stifle an emotional sob.

Luc seemed to be holding himself very still. And then he said, 'I've been cynical and mistrustful for a long time. I thought I knew women—knew how to handle them. I had no expectations, nor did I want anything more after Maria had burnt me. Until I met you. Within days you shattered every wall I'd built around myself. Every time I thought I had you in my sights, conforming to what I expected, you'd turn everything—*me*—on its head. You've turned my life upside down and inside out. And I thought I didn't want that. That I didn't need it.'

His mouth twisted and he looked disgusted.

'I sleep-walked through the last two weeks of hell, trying to convince myself of that. I crossed the globe twice in an effort to stay out of your orbit. And then in New York, when I saw you under siege on the news, I felt as if someone had shocked me back to life. The thought of you alone…the thought of something happening to you…I couldn't bear it.'

He took a deep breath.

'I love you. Just that. I love you, but those words can't even begin to convey the depth and breadth of how much I love you. I want to start over—right here and now. Wipe the slate clean. I want to seduce you all over again, and I'm warning you now that I'll play dirty if you resist.'

Feeling very shaky, Jesse said, 'How do you know this isn't just Stockhausen Syndrome…or whatever it is?'

Luc smiled. 'It's not Stock*holm* Syndrome. Apart from getting me here rather ingeniously, you were a pretty rubbish kidnapper.'

Jesse could see the nerves behind his smile, and it cracked her heart open. She believed him. 'So how do we start again?'

He held out a hand and said, 'I'm Luc...'

Jesse didn't wait. She flew across the space dividing them and straight into Luc's arms, legs wrapped around his waist, arms around his neck. The impact drove him back, but he held firm, arms like steel around her waist.

She finally pulled back, smiled through her tears and said, 'Hi, I'm Jesse.'

Luc smiled a sexy smile, and she could see his innate cocky confidence returning.

'You're a bit eager, aren't you? But I think I like it.'

Suddenly Jesse was serious. She cupped Luc's face with her hands and pressed a kiss to his mouth. She drew back. 'It terrifies me to admit it, but I love you too, Luc Sanchis. I think I love you more than life itself.'

Luc mock-groaned, but she could feel the effect of her words as his chest swelled against hers. 'Only *think*? That's not good enough. I think you need some serious convincing...'

Jesse pressed kisses down Luc's neck as he started walking out of the den and up the stairs. She said, 'Try to convince me, Sanchis. See how far it gets you.'

Luc growled softly. 'I've already got you, Moriarty, and I'm never letting you go again.'

Jesse looked up at him as he laid her back on the bed and touched his jaw with her hand. Her voice was husky. 'Is that a promise, Sanchis?'

'Yes,' he said briskly, ripping off his polo shirt before divesting Jesse of her sandals and trousers. His impatient hands were soon on her top, lifting it up. 'And how many times have I told you we've gone way beyond second names?'

When her top had sailed off, to land on the floor somewhere, Jesse wrapped her arms around Luc's neck and dragged him over her, spreading her legs so she could feel him hard against her.

Luc stopped moving for a moment and Jesse rolled her hips. He cursed softly and then said, 'Jesse Sanchis—now, there's a name…'

Jesse stilled, her heart tripping. She looked at Luc and felt dizzy. 'I might need convincing of that too. I'm very attached to Moriarty, and the way you say it…'

Luc pulled down one cup of her bra, thumbing her nipple. He looked at her, and at the hectic colour rising in her face, and his heart swelled with awe and adoration for this woman.

'That's a lot of convincing I have to do… I think we'll have to resign ourselves to the fact that we may be on this island for some time…'

Jesse smiled, and it wobbled precariously. 'That's fine by me. Take all the time you need.'

*A Year Later…*

Luc sat back in his chair at his desk and stretched. Dusk was settling over London outside. He glanced at his watch and stood up, taking his jacket in his hand. He left his office after bidding his secretary, Deborah, good evening and took the elevator down two floors.

When he stepped out he saw the glossy sign which read 'JMS Games Ltd'. *Jesse Moriarty Sanchis*. Though for everyday purposes she went by Jesse Sanchis.

She'd restructured her company in the previous year, to accommodate what she really wanted to focus on, and had moved her offices into Luc's building. The only problem with that was there was plenty of potential for distraction—which Jesse had become very adept at.

They'd sold her apartment and his townhouse to buy a house in Richmond with a huge garden, which a much bigger Tigger now patrolled with all the possessiveness of a very well loved cat.

Luc went and stood at the door to Jesse's office and smiled. Her hair was almost to her shoulders now, and pulled up in a loose bun with tendrils trailing down her neck. She was sitting cross-legged on the floor, surrounded by a group of teenagers, and she was saying passionately, 'It's the higher hidden level which you only reach by achieving a certain score that makes it so brilliant. It'll be a word-of-mouth-thing—like an urban legend…'

Jesse stopped when she felt that deliciously familiar tingle of awareness and saw a few of her focus group's eyes go over her head. She savoured this moment each day when Luc would wait for her—unless, of course, she went up to wait for him… She got hot just thinking about what invariably happened in those situations.

The kids started to pack up their things, and Jesse swivelled around on the floor and held out her hands to Luc, who came forward to pull her up.

He put a possessive hand on the seven-months-pregnant belly under her smock top. 'Much movement?'

She rolled her eyes and put her hand over his, savouring the intensity of his gaze—for *her*. It never failed to take away her breath. 'Unbelievable. I think it must have been the chilli in the sandwich I had at lunch.'

Luc teased, 'My wife, the gourmand…'

Mock-injured, Jesse said, 'I have never claimed a sophisticated palate.'

Luc grabbed Jesse's hand, suddenly wanting to be alone with her, and all but dragged her from the room.

She called back, 'Bye, guys, see you same time next week.'

They chorused, 'Bye, Jesse—bye, Mr Sanchis.'

When they were in Luc's car, and Jesse was curled into

his side, Luc said, 'Why do those kids insist on calling me Mr Sanchis?'

Jesse smiled and affected a note of disbelief when she spoke. 'Because for some reason they find you intimidating.'

'*You* never found me intimidating,' he grumbled good-naturedly.

Jesse curled into him even more and Luc tightened his arm around her. She relished the intensely physical and tactile nature of their relationship.

He kissed the top of her head after a few seconds' silence and said, 'Okay?'

Jesse nodded. She knew what he was talking about, of course. Her father had been sent to gaol the day before for fifteen years—a landmark sentence for someone like him, partly due to the fact that Jesse had gone on the stand to testify against him. Something she couldn't ever have considered doing without Luc's support.

'I'm just happy it's finally over...but I'm sad too—for the loss of something I never had. And I'm sad for your father, and my mother.'

Luc tipped her face up and pressed a kiss to her mouth. 'No more sadness. I won't allow it.'

Jesse smiled up at her husband and their baby kicked in her belly. She took his hand and put it there, so he could feel the kicks too.

No, there was no need for sadness any more.

\* \* \* \* \*

# MILLS & BOON®
## Book Club

# 2 Free Books!

## Get your free books now at
## www.millsandboon.co.uk/freebookoffer

---

## Or fill in the form below and post it back to us

**THE MILLS & BOON® BOOK CLUB™—HERE'S HOW IT WORKS:** Accepting your free books places you under no obligation to buy anything. You may keep the books and return the despatch note marked 'Cancel'. If we do not hear from you, about a month later we'll send you 4 brand-new stories from the Modern™ series priced at £3.49* each. There is no extra charge for post and packaging. You may cancel at any time, otherwise we will send you 4 stories a month which you may purchase or return to us—the choice is yours. *Terms and prices subject to change without notice. Offer valid in UK only. Applicants must be 18 or over. Offer expires 31st January 2013. **For all terms and conditions, please go to www.millsandboon.co.uk/freebookoffer**

Mrs/Miss/Ms/Mr (please circle)

First Name

Surname

Address

Postcode

E-mail

Send this completed page to: Mills & Boon Book Club, Free Book Offer, FREEPOST NAT 10298, Richmond, Surrey, TW9 1BR

---

Find out more at
**www.millsandboon.co.uk/freebookoffer**

*Visit us Online*

0712/P2YEA

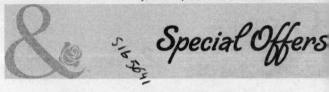